AF432151

The Holy Ache of the Unbecoming

The Holy Ache of the Unbecoming

Laughton J. Collins, Jr.

Published by Requiem Press.

https://requiempress.weebly.com/
https://www.laughtoncollinsjr.com

A Requiem Press Book

ISBN: 979-8-9928855-7-6

Contents

The Holy Ache of the Unbecoming

Part I

Chapter 1

The oppressive weight of the afternoon sun pressed down without mercy upon Victory Plaza. Baking the cracked concrete until heat shimmered in visible waves that distorted the edges of buildings and the figures of the crowd.

This vast public space, a sprawling expanse of worn stone and struggling patches of grass, had not always borne this name. A generation ago, it had been Unity Plaza, a place for festivals, markets, and lovers' rendezvous. The old fountain, now dry and filled with litter, had once cascaded with water, its basin a popular spot for children to cool their feet in the summer. The Leader, upon his rise, had declared that 'Unity' was a weak, passive concept, a relic of a compromising past. 'Victory,' however, was active, decisive, and belonged solely to him and his followers. With a stroke of a pen, Unity was erased, and Victory was imposed. The old plaques were pried from the walls of surrounding buildings and replaced with new, sharper-edged lettering. Now, the plaza was used for his rallies, a stage for his power, though on non-rally days, a strange, hollow normalcy returned. People still crossed it on their way to work. Some, perhaps out of habit or defiance, still sat on the few remaining benches to eat a meager lunch. The ghost of the plaza's former self lingering like a faint scent on the air.

Mira shifted her weight from one aching foot to the other, a dull and persistent throb radiating through her worn-down shoes from the long hours of standing motionless amidst the press of bodies. The dense and impenetrable wall of people around her seemed to generate its own thermal energy. It was a collective body heat that felt suffocating in the still air. A slick film of sweat gathered at the nape of her neck, tracing an itchy path beneath the coarse fabric of her collar.

1

From her position in the crowd, Mira could just see the top of the Tower of Song piercing the hazy skyline. Even from this distance, its melody was a faint, almost subconscious thread woven through the murmur of the masses. It was a haunting, wordless aria today, a solo voice that seemed to speak of a beauty and a sorrow so profound it made her heart ache. She saw others nearby subtly tilting their heads, listening without seeming to listen, their eyes growing distant. The Tower's call was a constant in the city, a siren song of a world that felt more authentic than the one they were forced to stand in. For a moment, the crowd's fervor seemed to waver, soothed by the distant music, and Mira felt a pang of shared longing. But then the loudspeakers on the poles crackled to life, and the Tower's melody was brutally drowned out by the regime's harsh, pre-recorded fanfare. The spell was broken; the crowd's attention was violently wrenched back to the stage.

She kept one hand buried deep within her coat pocket. Her fingers clutching the small photograph with a desperate and private intensity. Her thumb moving in a slow and rhythmic motion across its worn and softened edges as if offering a silent and tactile prayer to the fading image. That bright and beautiful smile was now just a ghost captured in faded color. A memory from his seventh year that existed in a lifetime before he vanished from the world eleven months ago. The paper itself feeling dangerously fragile in her grasp, as thin and fleeting as the hope she tried to maintain against the relentless tide of days.

Overhead, the loudspeakers mounted on metal poles emitted a sudden and violent crackle of static that cut through the murmur of the crowd. The entire crowd seemed to shuffle forward as one single organism. A low and eager murmur building swiftly into a wave of expectation that washed over the plaza. Every head turned in perfect unison toward the empty stage draped in banners of a single and solid color. He simply appeared then, stepping into the harsh and unforgiving light without any ceremony. The Leader materializing as if willed into being by the crowd's collective desire, flanked on all sides by a group of men wearing identical dark suits with faces that were a collection of blank and expressionless masks. Their eyes performing a continuous and unsmiling scan of the assembled masses.

The man who took the stage was a study in contrived perfection. His hair, that famous dull sienna, was immaculate, swept into a style that defied both the heat and the wind, a helmet of hairspray and willpower. It was the hair of a man decades younger, and the unnatural vigor it suggested was echoed in his posture and his strangely smooth, tight skin. He moved with a slouching, rolling gait that he seemed to believe conveyed strength, but which to Mira looked like the entitled swagger of a man who had never been told 'no'. He paused, bathing in the adulation, his small, pale hands raised. He did not wave; he merely presented himself for approval, a product to be adored. His face was fixed in a familiar expression: a slight, smug frown, the corners of his mouth turned down as if he alone could smell the nation's decay and found it personally offensive. He was the antithesis of the humble public servant; he was a king, a messiah, a brand, and he demanded worship, not respect. This was the antichrist of the modern age, not a figure of biblical horror but a television personality who had weaponized grievance and narcissism, wrapping a dictatorship in the flag and selling it back to the people as populism.

The Leader raised both of his hands into the air with a slow and deliberate motion, and an instant and absolute silence fell across the thousands of people. A silence so complete it felt heavier than the heat. He stood completely motionless under the glare of the lights. A figure of severe simplicity in his crisp and unadorned gray uniform that bore no insignia or medals of any kind. His face remarkably smooth and unlined for a man of his reported age. His hair was a dull and flat shade of sienna, each strand combed into a state of perfect and unyielding order. Most unnerving of all was the complete absence of sweat upon his brow despite the sweltering and oppressive heat that weighed upon everyone else. He lowered his hands back to his sides with an economical grace and then he began to speak. His voice amplified to reach every corner of the plaza yet retaining its calm and measured clarity. A voice that carried across the great distance without any apparent effort or strain, devoid of any raw emotion. Just words delivered with a chilling and precise calculation.

He began with a single word, allowing it to hang in the thick air as a verbal claim of ownership over the people standing before him. "People." He paused, letting the simple address settle over them, a single word that felt both inclusive and possessive. "Look around you at this very place." His gaze made a slow and theatrical sweep across the façades of the buildings that lined the square, buildings that showed clear signs of decay and neglect. "See the undeniable decay for what it truly is? See the pervasive weakness that has taken root?" His cold eyes moved over the crowd. Mira felt the sensation of his gaze passing over her like a sudden and unwelcome draft of frigid air. "A sickness of disorder choked us for a generation." His level tone never changed, stating these things as simple and irrefutable facts. "A plague of indecision crippled every one of our institutions. Foreign hands pulled our strings for their own amusement." He let that image linger for a moment before delivering the next line. "That pathetic time is now officially finished."

He leaned into the microphone, his voice dropping to a conspiratorial tone that was somehow still projected to the back of the plaza. "They don't want you to know the truth. The lying historians, the failing old media—they want to hide our greatness. But we have our own history now. A true history." He gestured vaguely east, toward the city's administrative district. "From the great Hall of Historical Corrections, we are reclaiming our past! We are throwing out the fake news of the losers and the haters and we are writing a new story, a winning story, the true story of our nation!" The crowd roared its approval at the name. The Hall was where inconvenient facts went to die and where glorious, flattering fictions were born, given the weight of law. To question its bulletins was not dissent; it was heresy.

A sharp and sudden cheer erupted from the throats of the crowd, a percussive blast of sound that felt violent in its intensity. Fists punching upward into the smoky air, a forest of arms moving in time with the chant. "Finished! Finished! Finished!" Mira kept her own hands tightly within her pockets. One wrapped around the photo, the other curled into a tense and hidden fist, watching the Leader's unnatural stillness, a quality that unnerved her far more than any shouted passion ever could. He did not join the chant or acknowledge it in any way; he simply waited, a predator allowing the noise to die down of its own accord before he continued. "We must now build everything anew from the ground up." His words cut through the fading echoes with surgical precision. "We will now demand a new and unassailable strength from every citizen. We will now demand a single and unifying purpose for our nation. We will now demand real and lasting Change."

The crowd roared its approval, the word becoming a weapon that was chanted with increasing volume. "Change! Change! Change!" The sound pounded against Mira's ears, a physical pressure that made her head ache. The word itself feeling hollow and meaningless in this context. *Change.* What did that word even mean here, now? The buildings visible behind the stage continued their slow crumble into dust. The air everyone breathed still carried the familiar taste of dust and coal smoke from the outdated factories on the city's edge. Her son was still just as gone today as he was yesterday. "Progress can no longer be a simple request from the people." The Leader continued, his hands remaining still at his sides. "Progress is now a direct command from the highest authority. It is our collective command. It is your individual command. Together, as one united body, we will forge a new and undeniable Progress."

"And to ensure this progress, we have the best people," he announced, his chest swelling. "So strong, so smart. The tremendous minds at the Bureau of Counter Intelligence are ensuring our children are taught the right things, the strong things, not the weak, globalist nonsense of the past." A few cheers rose, though they seemed more confused this time. Everyone knew the BCI was where good teachers went to be "re-educated" and where the curriculum was stripped of anything resembling critical thought. It was an open secret that the only qualification for a high-ranking position there was unwavering loyalty to The Leader, not any aptitude for education. He smirked, a knowing, ugly little twist of the lips. "And my cabinet! The incredible patriots in the Bureau of Belligerent Blunder Heads—though they want me to stop calling them that, can you believe it?" He paused for the laughter that dutifully rippled through the crowd. "They are the best! So tough, so ready to fight. They don't get caught up in the details. They just get things done. They're blunderheads, but they're *my* blunderheads." The laughter grew louder, more desperate. This was part of the ritual: his confidants were buffoons, and he loved them for it, because their buffoonery depended entirely on him. It was a public display of dominance. Proving he could elevate the most incompetent to the highest offices, and no one could stop him.

The crowd answered him as a single voice, a wave of sound that felt both eager and desperate. "Progress! Progress! Progress!" Mira observed the raw fervor etched onto the faces nearest to her. Their eyes were wide with a kind of hungry belief, their lips moving in perfect sync with the official slogans. A woman standing beside her had begun to weep openly. Tears cutting clean tracks through the layer of grime on her cheeks. Her voice cracking with the force of the chant. Mira felt nothing within her own chest but a hollow and expanding sense of dread. The words themselves felt completely empty to her, hollow shells that produced a sound but carried no meaning. Meaningless noises bouncing off the cracked walls of the city. She looked past the Leader himself, past the stage and its banners, to the tired buildings that framed the plaza, windows broken and boarded up, old brickwork crumbling into the alleys below. Graffiti marred the lower walls, though older slogans had been painted over in a hurry. Faded posters from elections past clung to the walls, their torn edges flapping in the slight breeze, showing the Leader's face from years ago, younger and smiling. A promise that now seemed to mock the present decay, which felt deeper and more ingrained than ever before.

The Leader spoke then of national unity, of the necessity of shared sacrifice, of the enemies that supposedly hid within their borders and the ones that threatened from beyond. He spoke of a great national purification, of the urgent need to remove the rotten timbers that weakened the entire structure of the republic. His voice never rose in volume and never wavered in its calm and steady delivery. It was this very calmness, this absolute and total control, that Mira understood as the real and present danger. She felt it as a physical pressure, a subtle tightening around her throat, an invisible velvet noose. This was not the passion of a believer; it was the cold and precise calculation of a machine grinding inexorably forward. He spoke of loyalty, the absolute and non-negotiable loyalty required from every citizen, the very foundation of the new republic he was building. He spoke of constant vigilance, of the duty to report any doubt, to report any dissent, to report anything or anyone that could hinder the sacred march of Progress.

"Trust must be earned through concrete action alone," he stated, his eyes narrowing a fraction. "Silence in the face of doubt will be interpreted as complicity. Complicity is nothing less than betrayal of the republic itself." The crowd absorbed this directive, nodding along, chanting their agreement when prompted. "Loyalty! Progress! Change!" Mira closed her eyes for a single second, blocking out the sight of him, and saw instead her son Ben's face with perfect clarity. The gap in his teeth from the tooth he lost at school. The small freckle just behind his ear. The particular way his nose would wrinkle up when he would laugh a real and genuine laugh. The official report had said he was a runaway, a conclusion they reached without any evidence. They said he was found drowned in the river, a case they closed without any questions asked. *Change. Progress.* They were just words, she understood, words designed to bury the truth under a mountain of official paperwork and patriotic slogans.

She opened her eyes again to the grim reality of the plaza. The Leader was still speaking, listing a series of achievements that sounded impressive but felt intangible. Production quotas had been met in certain sectors. Traitors to the state had been apprehended and would face justice. New regulations for public order and civic conduct would be announced soon. His words flowed like a stream of thick oil, smooth and slick, coating everything in a veneer of acceptable normality. A man standing near the front of the crowd, overcome by the heat and the pressure of the packed bodies, suddenly fainted, slumping toward the hard concrete. Security moved with a frightening efficiency. Two men in those same dark suits appearing instantly to drag him away from the view of the crowd, their actions silent and practiced. The Leader did not pause his speech for even a single syllable. The crowd itself barely seemed to notice the interruption, their chant continuing without a break. "Strength! Order! Progress!" Mira watched the empty spot where the man had fallen. Nothing was left behind but a faint scuff mark on the concrete that was quickly swallowed by the shifting of a hundred feet. He had been removed, erased from the scene. Just like her son. Just like so many others she had heard about. Gone into the vast and hungry system without leaving a trace.

The Leader brought his address to its conclusion. "The future belongs entirely to us now." He spoke with a tone of finality. "You must seize it with your own hands. You must demand it with your own voice. You must become it with your every action. For Change. For Progress. For the Republic!" The final roar from the crowd shook the very foundations of the plaza. A deafening and sustained wave of sound that seemed to feed on its own energy. The Leader offered a single and sharp nod in acknowledgment, a gesture that was both a thank you and a dismissal. He turned on his heel with military precision and walked off the stage without a backward glance. His dark-suited guards closing ranks around him until he disappeared entirely into the deep shadows behind the scaffolding.

The motorcade that would whisk him away was waiting, a line of black vehicles that looked like predatory insects. They wouldn't take him to a government building or an office. They would speed through the increasingly dilapidated city streets toward the very edge, where the city lights gave way to a profound darkness. There, surrounded by an immense wall and shrouded in isolation, stood The

Light House. It was his residence, a fortress of ego perpetually illuminated by blinding, wasteful spotlights that bleached the surrounding land, a lighthouse that warned of the rocks of his own personality rather than guiding anyone to safety. He would retreat there, to a world of gold-plated fixtures and televisions endlessly playing his own speeches, surrounded by sycophants from the Bureau of Belligerent Blunder Heads, utterly divorced from the crumbling reality of the nation he ruled.

The recorded fanfare blared once more, its triumphant melody sounding hollow and false now. The crowd began its slow process of dispersal. People turning away with a reluctant slowness, the shared energy of the event lingering in the air around them. People talked to one another in excited and relieved tones, their faces flushed with a sense of purpose. Mira remained utterly still for a long moment, allowing the current of bodies to flow around her as if she were a stone in a river. She felt numb inside, the hollow dread having now solidified into something hard and cold and permanent within her gut. The Leader's calm certainty was not reassuring; it was the greatest threat she could imagine. A promise of more erasure, more silence, more vanished sons and daughters, all in the name of an empty ideal. She finally looked down at her own feet, at the concrete littered with the debris of the gathering. Cigarette butts, scraps of paper, trampled leaflets bearing the Leader's face. And everywhere, a fine and gray ash.

The ash drifted in lazy tendrils from the dozen braziers that lined the plaza's perimeter, iron barrels where cheap coal burned day and night. They marked the official rally space, providing a thin and inadequate heat but mostly producing a constant and acrid smoke that stained the air. Flakes of ash drifted on the thermal currents, settling on shoulders and hair and the ground below. Mira watched a single and perfect flake land near the scuffed toe of her worn shoe. She knelt down on the hard ground, ignoring the jostling legs of the departing crowd moving past her. From her worn canvas bag, she pulled the small mason jar, its glass cool to the touch, its lid screwed on tightly. A strip of faded masking tape was affixed to the lid, a single word written upon it in her own faint pencil script: *November.*

She unscrewed the metal lid, the threaded ring catching for a second on the skin of her thumb. She held the jar low and close to the ground, using the lid itself as a tiny dustpan. She began to sweep the ash toward it, gathering the gray powder, which was fine as flour and stained the concrete where it lay. She performed this task with a meticulous care, each motion slow and deliberate. Her knuckles brushed against the gritty surface of the plaza. She focused all her attention on this simple action, blocking out the residual noise of the crowd, the fading echoes of the chants inside her own mind. *Change. Progress.* They were just words. This ash was real. It was solid. It was evidence. Not a word, not a promise. This was what truly remained after the fire died down. After the speech ended. After the vanished were forgotten. This silent and gray residue.

She swept another small patch of ash into her makeshift pan, this one nearer to the leg of a brazier where the residue was thicker and darker. She carefully tipped it into the mouth of the jar, watching the fine powder cascade down to form a growing pile at the bottom. She remembered the very first jar she had filled on a cold November night. The night her son did not come home. The night the new precinct commander gave his speech promising safety and order and progress. The braziers had burned that night, too, their smoke mixing with the fog. She had scooped the ash from the ground because she needed to hold something real and tangible in the face of words that meant nothing, when her hands would otherwise have been completely empty.

She added another careful sweep of ash to the collection. The jar's bottom was now covered by a quarter-inch of the gray material. She continued her work, methodical and unnoticed in the quickly thinning crowd. People hurried past her, eager to leave, to forget the event or to celebrate it in private. A heavy black boot scuffed the concrete very near her hand. A security guard stood over her, tall and imposing in his neat uniform. His eyes performed a quick and professional scan of the area before looking down at her, at the woman kneeling to sweep ash into a small glass jar. His gaze lingered for a moment, flat and assessing, devoid of any curiosity. Then it moved on. She was not chanting, she was not cheering, but she was not causing a disturbance either. She was just a woman gathering dirt, a harmless and insignificant creature. He walked on without saying a word.

Mira allowed herself a slow and quiet breath. She swept more of the ash into her jar. Her fingers were now stained a dirty gray, the powder smudged into her skin. The jar gained a little more weight, a little more substance with each addition. *November*. The month of endings. The month when the cold truly settled in for the long duration. She thought of her son then. Not the official story of the runaway. Not the report of the river, but of his actual self. His fear of the dark that required a nightlight. His cherished collection of smooth stones from the riverbank. The specific sound of his laughter echoing through their tiny kitchen. All of it was gone, vanished into the system's vast and hungry silence. Just like the man who was dragged away. Just like the faded posters. Just like the promises made on this very spot.

The Leader's own words echoed in the hollow space he had carved out inside her. *Silence is complicity*. He was right, but not in the way he meant it. Her silence now was not a complicity with his power; it was a preservation of her own. It was a different kind of silence. A quiet and private space where she could hold onto what was real, onto what was truly left. She swept the last patch of ash within her reach, carefully tipping the contents of the lid into the jar and watching the final particles settle. She screwed the lid back on tightly, sealing the contents away from the world. She wiped her gray fingers on the dark fabric of her coat, leaving faint streaks behind. She stood up, her knees protesting the movement with a sharp ache.

The plaza was nearly empty now, populated only by a few slow-moving stragglers. The clean-up crews were already moving in. Men dressed in drab overalls sweeping the ground with wide brooms, hosing down sections of concrete, erasing all the footprints, the litter and any other evidence that a crowd had ever been here. The braziers continued to smoke, sending their thin gray plumes up into the dull and uncaring sky. Mira held the sealed jar in her hand, feeling its slight but meaningful weight, the gritty residue that had settled under the rim of the lid. She looked at the label one more time. *November.* It was not just for her son. It was for the fear, for the lies, for the Leader's cold and calculating eyes, for the crowd's eager roar, for the act of vanishing itself. All of it was reduced to this simple substance. *Ash.* A memory made solid. A quiet and defiant act contained within a glass jar.

She placed the jar carefully back into her canvas bag, letting it rest beside the photograph of her son. She adjusted the collar of her coat against a sudden chill that the evening air was bringing and turned her back on Victory Plaza. Her steps away from the square were slow and heavy but also deliberate. Each one carrying her home toward the cramped apartment that felt too large without him. Toward the silence that was not complicity. Toward the stubborn and necessary act of holding on, of remembering, one jar of ash at a time. The city sounds began to return as the last of the rally noise faded, the normal hum of life asserting itself, and she walked into that hum, a single figure carrying a small and heavy truth away from the altar of ashes. The evening was closing in around the buildings, and the lights in the windows of the apartments she passed were beginning to flicker on. Each one a small and distant promise of shelter, of a private world away from the chants and the speeches. A world where different truths could be held, however fragilely, in the quiet of one's own hands.

Her route home took her on a winding path through the city's decaying heart. She deliberately avoided the Street of the Pioneers, where the new Hall of Historical Corrections stood, its neoclassical façade hiding the labyrinth of offices where teams of bureaucrats diligently scrubbed the past clean. She could almost feel the lies radiating from its marble walls. Instead, she cut through a narrow alley, the sound of her footsteps echoing. From here, she could hear it—a faint, impossibly complex saxophone riff weaving through the damp air. It was coming from The Jazz Club, a basement establishment tucked beneath a derelict hotel. Its existence was tolerated, for now, a pressure valve for the city's creative energy. The music was a language of freedom and improvisation. The absolute opposite of the rigid, pre-approved fanfares of the regime. It was a testament to something that couldn't be easily stamped out.

As she turned onto her own street, she passed the public library. A new sign, freshly hung, declared it "The Library of Errors." The windows were dark. It had been closed for months, its contents undergoing "review." Everyone knew the real books—the novels, the poetry, the histories that contradicted the Hall's bulletins—were being pulped. Soon it would reopen, its shelves filled with approved texts: biographies of The Leader, technical manuals, and dense ideological texts that all somehow proved the infallibility of the regime. A library of wrong answers to false questions.

She finally reached her building, her hand closing around the key in her pocket. But her mind was not on the jars or the quiet apartment. It was on a word, whispered only in the most trusted of company: *The Undercurrent*. She had heard it first from her sister, Lena, who had heard it from a friend who worked in the utilities department. It was a name for the faint hope, the silent network of those who had not been fooled. There were no leaders, no manifestos. Just a shared look, a helping hand, a piece of real information passed along. It was what her ash-gathering was—a small part of that undercurrent. A quiet resistance that flowed beneath the surface of obedience, waiting, persisting. The Leader could command the plaza, but he could not command the human spirit that hid in the cracks and shadows.

She reached her own building and climbed the stairs, each step a familiar and weary ascent. The door to her apartment opened with its familiar click, and the silence inside welcomed her. It was a different silence from the one in the plaza, a silence that was hers alone. She went to the shelf, a simple plank of wood nailed to the wall, and there they stood: eleven mason jars, each with a label, each holding the residue of a month since her son's disappearance. *January, February, March, April, May, June,* July, *August,*

September, October. She placed the new jar at the end of the line. *November.* She set the photograph of her son on the shelf in front of the jars, his face smiling at the row of gray emptiness. She stood there for a long time, looking at the jars, looking at the photograph, as the light from the window faded and the room grew dark around her.

A sound came from downstairs. A door slamming shut with more force than usual, followed by footsteps on the stairs that were fast and urgent, someone running up to her door. The doorknob turned before she could move to answer it, and the door flew open to reveal her sister standing in the doorway. Her face was pale and her eyes wide with a fear that was immediately noticeable. She was breathing hard from the climb, one hand pressed to her chest as if to steady her racing heart. She looked at Mira, then her eyes darted to the shelf of ash jars, her mouth opening but no sound coming out. She took a step into the room, her hand outstretched, and in it was a small and gray piece of paper that Mira recognized instantly. She had seen one before. It was a receipt.

Chapter 2

The chill that permeated the air outside had seeped into the very walls of Mira's apartment, a deep and penetrating cold that the feeble radiator could not hope to overcome. Lena stood there for a moment just inside the door, allowing the familiar silence of the small space to envelop her, a stark contrast to the roaring crowd and the Leader's amplified voice that still echoed faintly in her memory. Her fingers, stiff and cold, went through the practiced motions of removing her coat and hanging it on the solitary hook, her movements slow and deliberate as if she were moving through water. She was breathing in short, ragged gasps, her chest heaving as she clutched a worn handbag tight against her stomach. The cold air from the hallway rushed in with her, carrying the scent of damp wool and fear.

"He's gone," Lena rasped, the words barely audible, torn from a throat raw with crying. "They took him. Last night."

The words hung in the small space between them, sharp and cold. Mira closed the door slowly, the click of the lock sounding like a verdict. She guided her sister further into the room, away from the door, but Lena remained standing, trembling, her gaze darting around the room without truly seeing it.

"Who took him?" Mira asked, her voice low and steady, though she already knew the answer. "When?"

"Men came," Lena whispered, her hands beginning to tremble uncontrollably. She fumbled with the clasp of her handbag, her fingers seeming to refuse to work properly. "Late. After curfew. They pounded on the door." She finally managed to get the clasp open and pulled out a single piece of paper, thrusting it toward Mira as if it were something that burned her fingers. "They had papers. Official. Stamped. They said...questioning. About his work. They didn't say where."

Mira took the paper. It was a standard sheet of cheap gray pulp, the kind used for countless bureaucratic forms. At the top was a serial number. Below it, stark and impersonal, were typed lines of text:

Detainee: Tomasz Varga
Reason: Administrative Review
(Work Record Discrepancy - Sector 7)
Authority: Order Compliance Bureau - Precinct 5
Receiving Officer: ID# 86-47 (Signature Illegible)
Date/Time: 23:47, Last Night
Next of Kin Notified: N/A (Per Directive 7-C)

There was no location listed. No duration for the review. No information on how to contact anyone. It was a receipt for a human being, a transaction slip that acknowledged a person had been taken into custody while offering no details about his whereabouts or his future.

"He argued with them," Lena continued, her voice gaining a little strength now, fueled by a desperate need to tell the story, to make it real. "Said it was a mistake. That his records were clean. That he filed everything on time. Always." Her voice cracked on the last word. "They didn't listen. They just...took him. Put their hands on him. Took him away in a van with black windows." She stared at the receipt in Mira's hand. "This is all they left. This...this thing."

Mira refolded the paper carefully along its original creases, the action methodical, a way to keep her own hands from shaking. She handed it back to her sister. "Did they search the apartment?"

Lena nodded, a jerky, broken motion. "Tore through everything. Drawers emptied. Cupboards opened. They looked behind pictures. Under the mattress. Took his work tablet. His personal notebook." She wiped her nose with the back of her hand, a helpless, childlike gesture. "They found nothing. There was nothing *to* find. He was clean."

The silence that followed was thick and heavy, broken only by the faint hiss of the radiator. Lena's shoulders slumped, the initial surge of panicked energy leaving her. "What do I do?" she asked, the question was a plea, hollow and hopeless.

Mira knew the script. She had lived it herself. "You go to the Precinct Office," she said, her voice flat. "The one on Sovereign Avenue. You stand in line. The line will be long. You will wait for hours. You will show them the receipt. You will ask for a status report."

Lena's eyes searched her sister's face, looking for something that wasn't there. "And then? What will they say?"

"They will take the paper. They will look at the number. They will type it into a machine. They will tell you the review is ongoing. They will tell you to go home. To wait." Mira delivered the instructions without emotion, each sentence a stone dropped into a deep well.

"Wait for what?" Lena's voice was a whisper now, all the fight gone out of it.

"They will not say. They will never say. You will go back the next day. You will stand in the line again. You will do the same thing. Every day. You will do this until you stop going."

The terrible simplicity of it, the futility, settled over them both. Lena sank onto the single kitchen chair, the receipt clutched in her hand, her body seeming to fold in on itself under the weight of this new reality. Mira turned away from the sight of her sister's devastation, needing air, needing space. She walked to the window and slid it open, stepping out onto the small balcony.

The cold air hit her face like a slap, a sharp and cleansing shock after the stifling atmosphere of the apartment. The balcony was a tiny concrete slab, barely large enough for two people to stand on, overlooking a narrow alley of dank walls and overflowing bins. A few scraggly plants, a gift from Lena the previous spring, sat in cracked pots, most of them long since succumbed to neglect and the cold. Only one still showed any signs of life: a small rose bush, its stems thorny and bare except for a few dark green, waxy leaves and two last blooms.

The flowers were past their prime, their petals once a deep crimson now bruised a dark purple at the edges and fading to a sickly brown in the centers. They drooped heavily on their stems, beaten down by the wind and the rain, their beauty transformed into a kind of wounded dignity. One petal hung loose, ready to fall at the slightest touch. They looked, to Mira's eyes, like a reflection of everything around her: clinging to a semblance of life while slowly rotting at the core.

She reached out, not to smell them, but to touch them, to feel something other than the cold dread that had taken root in her stomach. Her finger traced the curve of a bruised petal, feeling its cool and velvety texture, its heartbreaking fragility. A thorn, sharp and black, hidden among the leaves, snagged the pad of her thumb. The pain was sudden and insistent, a bright, sharp signal from the world of the living.

She pulled her hand back and looked at her thumb. A single, perfect bead of blood welled up from the tiny puncture, a deep and vivid red against her pale skin. It swelled, trembling on the surface, a perfect and ominous jewel.

From inside the apartment, she could hear the muffled sound of Lena's quiet sobs, a soft, hopeless rhythm. The image of the receipt burned in her mind, its bureaucratic language a cold veil over the reality of a man being taken from his home. She thought of her son's smile, the Leader's sweatless face, the bleached posters on the streets, the mindless chant of the crowd. *Change. Progress.*

Her gaze shifted from her bleeding thumb to the mason jar inside, sitting on the shelf. *November.* The ash inside, gray and silent, represented her son's absence, her brother-in-law's absence, the nation's decay. All contained, labeled, and filed away.

The blood bead trembled on her thumb. Without conscious thought, without any plan, Mira moved. She stepped back inside, walked to the shelf, and picked up the November jar. She pressed her bleeding thumb directly against the cool glass, right over the handwritten label.

She smeared it. Deliberately. A single, dark streak across the faded pencil word. The blood was thick and opaque, covering the 'N', obscuring the 'v', marking the ash within with this new offering. It was a silent protest. A signature in blood on this altar of ashes. Not a shout, not a cry, but a stain. A mark. Evidence of pain. Her pain. Lena's pain. Tomasz's pain. Her son's pain.

She pulled her thumb away. The smear remained, a dark red brand on the clear glass over the gray powder inside. The thorn's tiny wound still wept a little blood. She did not wipe it away.

The glass door slid open behind her. Lena stood there, her eyes swollen and red, her face blotchy from crying. She held herself stiffly, trying to maintain some semblance of control. Her gaze went to Mira's hand, to the blood welling on her thumb, then to the jar, to the fresh, dark smear across *November*.

Lena took a deep breath. Her eyes locked with Mira's. No words passed between them. There were no words adequate for this moment. There was only the shared sight: the blood, the ash, the label, the silent and defiant mark that had been made.

Lena's lips pressed into a thin, hard line. She gave a single, tiny, almost imperceptible nod. Her eyes, which moments before had been pools of helpless grief, hardened. Not with hope, but with resolve. A different kind of silence had entered the room, one charged with a new and grim understanding.

She turned back into the apartment. "I need tea," she said, her voice raw but steady. "Strong tea."

Mira watched her go. She looked down at the jar in her hands. The blood was already darkening, drying into a permanent record. A new layer had been added to the memory. A promise had been written in pain. She placed the jar back on the shelf, beside the photograph of her son. The red streak faced the room, a stark contrast to the gray ash and the faded smile.

Lena filled the kettle and set it on the stove. The gas flame hissed to life with a blue spark. She got out two chipped mugs, her movements precise and focused, anchored by the simple, domestic task.

Mira sat down at the table, watching the kettle, waiting for the water to boil, waiting for the steam to rise. The silence between them was no longer empty. It was full of Tomasz's absence, full of her son's smile, full of the blood on the jar, full of the unspoken question that now hung in the steam-filled air between them. What would they do now? The water began to heat, and the first faint whisper of its coming boil filled the room.

The tea was bitter, brewed too long and without sugar, which had become a luxury. They drank it in silence, the hot liquid doing little to warm the cold knot of fear in Mira's stomach. Lena's hands shook as she held her mug, the receipt for her husband lying on the table between them like a dead thing.

"I have to go," Lena said finally, her voice hollow. "To the precinct. I have to stand in the line."

Mira nodded. There was no alternative. To not go would be to mark yourself, to invite the very scrutiny that had taken Tomasz. "I'll come with you," she said.

Lena looked up, with gratitude and despair in her eyes. "You don't have to."

"I know."

They left the apartment together, stepping out into the gray morning. The walk to Sovereign Avenue was long and silent. The city seemed quieter than usual, the normal sounds of life muted, as if it too were holding its breath. They passed the Cathedral of Silence. Its immense doors were shut, as always. No one ever seemed to go in or out. Mira had heard the stories, of course. That inside, no matter how loud you screamed, no sound could be heard. It was a place of absolute auditory void, where confessions were extracted and souls were quieted. She shuddered and quickened her pace, pulling her coat tighter around her. The thought of Tomasz in such a place was unbearable.

Sovereign Avenue was broad and grim, lined with official buildings of stern, gray stone. The Precinct Office was at the end of the street, and even from a distance, they could see the line. It was exactly as Mira had described: long, slow-moving, and composed of people with the same hollow-eyed, fearful expression. They took their place at the end, joining the silent queue of the damned.

Hours passed. The line inched forward. Lena stood rigid, the receipt crumpled in her fist. Mira watched the people ahead of them reach the counter, speak a few words, and then leave, their shoulders slumped even further. No one ever left with good news.

As they waited, a woman in front of them, her face etched with a lifetime of hardship, turned slightly. She didn't look at them directly, but she spoke in a voice so low it was almost a whisper, meant only for their ears. "They took my boy last week. Welding apprentice. They said his torch was set wrong. Wasted state resources." She shook her head, a minute movement. "They'll say anything."

Lena took a breath. "Did you…have you heard anything?"

The woman's eyes flickered toward a security guard lounging by the door. "You don't hear," she murmured. "You just wait. But…look for the marks. On the walls. On the pavements. Near the drains. They point the way."

Mira's heart began to beat faster. "What marks?"

"The quiet ones," the woman said cryptically, before turning fully away from them as the line moved up. The conversation was over. She had taken a risk, and now she was retreating into the protective shell of anonymity.

Mira's mind raced. *The quiet ones. The Undercurrent.* This was it. This was a sign. It wasn't much, but it was a thread, however thin. It was something other than hopeless waiting.

Finally, it was Lena's turn. She approached the counter, a thick pane of scratched plexiglass, and handed the receipt to the clerk, a young man with a bored, vacant expression. He took it, typed the number into his terminal, and stared at the screen for a moment.

"Review is ongoing," he said in a monotone, not looking at her. "Next."

"But where is he?" Lena asked, her voice trembling. "Can I bring him anything? Clothes? Food?"

The clerk's eyes flicked up to hers, utterly devoid of empathy. "Next," he repeated, sliding the receipt back under the glass.

Lena stood frozen for a second before Mira gently took her arm and led her away. They walked out of the building and onto the street, the cold air feeling even colder after the stifling, fearful heat of the office.

"He didn't even look at me," Lena whispered. "It was like I wasn't even there."

"I know," Mira said, holding her sister's arm tightly. But her own mind was not on the clerk's indifference. It was on the woman's words. *Look for the marks.*

On the way back, Mira's eyes scanned the walls, the pavements, the gutters. She saw nothing but graffiti that had been painted over, posters for rallies, and cracks in the concrete. Then, as they turned down a narrow side street, she saw it. Faint, almost invisible, scratched into the paint on a drainpipe: a small, simple symbol. It looked like a wave, or a river current flowing underground.

She stopped, pulling Lena to a halt. She didn't say anything, just pointed. Lena followed her gaze, her eyes widening slightly in recognition. It was a message—a sign. They were not alone. The Undercurrent was real. It was here, in this very street, offering a silent, dangerous thread of connection.

They walked home in a different silence. It was no longer the silence of pure despair. It was the silence of a shared secret, a fragile, terrifying hope. The blood on the jar was a promise between them. And now, this mark on the wall was a promise from the world. The fight was not over. It had just become quieter, deeper, and more dangerous.

Chapter 3

The air within the *Daily Beacon* pressroom carried a distinct and permanent flavor of ink and dust, underpinned by something else entirely. A sour and metallic taste that might have been defeat or perhaps just the slow decomposition of cheap paper. Elias stood at his assigned desk with its metal frame and chipped laminate top. A terminal with keys worn smooth by endless use sitting before him alongside a stack of fresh pulp sheets. The morning briefing sheet lay flat next to his keyboard, its headlines pre-approved by the Central Propaganda Directorate and ready for his particular touch, for the polished syntax that would make the lies feel palatable to a weary populace.

He read the top directive printed in bold and uncompromising type. A statement about the Leader hailing a record harvest from Sector Seven despite global shortfalls. Elias knew the actual situation in Sector Seven because his own cousin lived and worked there; the last desperate letter he had received spoke only of crop blight, empty silos and deepening ration cuts. The approved words on the briefing sheet felt heavy and false in his mind, like stones he was meant to carry in his pocket as he went about his day, a constant reminder of his own participation in the great silencing of truth.

This directive, like all the others, hadn't originated from any editor with a shred of journalistic instinct. It had been faxed over on crisp, official letterhead from the *Hall of Historical Corrections*. The Hall didn't just approve stories; it authored reality. Its teams of "historical architects" worked in shifts, tirelessly rewriting events, scrubbing inconvenient people from photographs, and producing these daily bulletins that newspapers like the *Beacon* were legally mandated to publish verbatim. Elias pictured the Hall now: a monstrous, modern building of glass and steel, a deliberate contrast to the crumbling city around it. Inside, he imagined vast, climate-controlled archives where the actual past was stored, not to be studied, but to be systematically erased—names redacted from documents, dates altered, photographs scissored apart. The record harvest from Sector Seven was just the latest fiction to emerge from that factory of lies. A lie that would now, through his hands, be typeset and printed and delivered as truth. His terminal was merely the final, obedient conduit in a long pipeline of falsehood that started in the Hall's sterile laboratories.

His fingers moved over the keys with a practiced rhythm. Tapping out the required lies and polishing them until they shone with a fake and brittle optimism. He wrote about an unprecedented yield demonstrating the strength of new agrarian directives. He composed sentences about Sector Seven workers exemplifying progress through their discipline. Each word he typed felt like a small and quiet death, an obituary for a simple fact that had once been allowed to exist. He finished the piece, saved it and sent it to the editor's queue without a byline. No individual names were attached to the work anymore. Only the institution's name mattered now as a collective mouthpiece for the regime.

He pushed his chair back and the metal legs scraped against the concrete floor. A sound that echoed in the cavernous and nearly silent room where other journalists sat equally hunched over their own terminals, equally complicit in the great silencing. His assigned task was not yet complete for the day, for the real and unspoken work still waited for him in the basement archive. He walked past rows of silent terminals and past the empty desks where other kinds of writers had once sat, down a narrow stairwell where the air grew colder and danker by the step.

The smell of fresh ink faded away completely, replaced by the sharp and unpleasant tang of chemical preservatives and, beneath that, the faint and sweet scent of paper decay. The archive room itself was vast and imposing. With high ceilings lost in the gloom and metal shelves stretching away into the shadows. All of them packed tight with bound volumes of newspapers and reports and boxes of microfiche. A physical history of the time before the *Change*, before the *Progress*, before the Leader's smooth and sweatless face had come to dominate every front page.

A young man in gray overalls waited for him by the furnace room door, his face a careful blank, his eyes avoiding any direct contact. He held a clipboard and mumbled about Batch Seven being marked per directive, pointing towards a pallet stacked with old and stained cardboard boxes tied with rough twine. Elias nodded his understanding without speaking. The young man scurried back towards the light and the warmth upstairs, leaving him alone with the past. Elias unlocked the heavy furnace room door and pulled it open, a blast of heat immediately striking his face as the dull roar of the fire filled the small space. The furnace mouth was glowing a hungry orange.

He dragged the first heavy box inside, cut the twine and lifted the lid, watching as a cloud of dust puffed into the hot air carrying the smell of old paper and forgotten words. He pulled out a bound volume of the *Beacon* from five years prior and flipped through its pages, seeing headlines about real protests, actual shortages and genuine investigations. Words leaping out at him about corruption probes widening in the Infrastructure Ministry, audits revealing discrepancies in defense contracts and ministers resigning amidst allegations. These were the obituaries for facts that could not be allowed to live in the Leader's new world. Words that invited dangerous questions and corrosive doubt, words like corruption and probe and allegations that were now considered infectious and seditious.

Elias opened the furnace door wider until the heat seared his face. He tossed the entire volume into the flames, watching as they leapt up with yellow tongues to lick the dry paper, hungry and efficient. The pages blackened and curled and vanished into nothingness. The light of their truth becoming mere heat and then ash. The word *corruption* burning first in a brief flare before it was gone forever. He threw in another volume and then another. Working with a methodical rhythm, box after box, feeding the furnace and feeding the great silence. Burning the inconvenient past to rewrite history one fire at a time.

He reached into a particularly crumbling box that held not bound volumes but loose papers, internal memos, reports and shredded documents that had been diverted from pulping to this more final destination. He scooped up a great handful and tossed them towards the flames, watching them flutter like dying birds before vanishing into the orange glow. One small scrap caught the updraft and twisted back to land near his boot, a charred corner with torn edges that he almost kicked back into the fire out of habit. But a surviving fragment of text caught his eye, printed letters only half-burned, and he bent to pick it up, feeling it hot against his fingers.

The scrap was small and charred black along one edge, but the surviving words were clear and typewritten in capital letters, an incomplete sentence that read *"...WAS LIAR AND THIEF. EVIDENCE..."* with the rest of the message gone to ash. The sentence hung in the air around him, accusatory and final, a truth that had somehow escaped the fire and now felt like a physical punch. He looked from the roaring and oblivious furnace back down to the trembling scrap in his soot-stained fingers, wondering who had been the liar and thief and what evidence had been lost, all of it erased but for this ghost of an accusation.

He did not allow himself to think. He only acted, folding the scrap small and tight and pushing it deep into his trouser pocket. The rough paper scraped against his leg, a tiny and dangerous secret ember against the consuming fire. He threw the rest of the loose papers into the furnace and watched them vanish completely. He slammed the heavy door shut, muting the roar and lessening the heat. He leaned against the grimy wall to catch his breath. The scrap in his pocket feeling like a live coal that might burn through the fabric. He pulled out a rag to wipe his hands, the black soot smearing into gray. His palms now stained in a way that felt akin to the blood and ash that marked Mira's jar, stained with secrets and complicity.

Back at his desk upstairs, his terminal screen glowed with a new assignment waiting. A directive to commemorate one year of the Progress Initiative with a focus on unity and sacrifice and renewed purpose. He sat down heavily and let his fingers hover over the keys, feeling them cold and stiff and unwilling. His gaze drifted instead to the bottom left drawer of his desk. He pulled it open to reveal not pens or paper clips but a small stack of letters. All in envelopes addressed in a familiar and looping hand he knew belonged to his daughter. The letters were postmarked from the Western College District. He realized with a sinking heart that he had not opened the last three she had sent, finding himself unable to face the words he knew they would contain.

He picked up the most recent envelope and pulled out the flimsy cheap paper within. His daughter's neat, precise and angry writing filling the page with accusations he knew he deserved. She asked if he even read her letters anymore, if he even cared. She mentioned a propaganda film he had written the narration for that praised the very quotas starving Sector Seven. She said her mother would not recognize the man he had become. He traced her signature with a soot-stained finger, seeing the tight loops of her controlled fury. Each letter a sharp and deserved accusation. He saw her face with her mother's eyes full of the disappointment he had earned. He put the letter down without reading the others, their words were like knives turning in the wound of his own silence. He looked back at the terminal screen where the cursor blinked, waiting and demanding more lies.

He thought of the scrap in his pocket with its damning fragment "...*WAS LIAR*..." He thought of his daughter's question about when the burning would stop. Then he placed his hands on the keys and took a breath of the sour air and began to type. He formed the hollow and glittering shells of sentences about one year of progress being a testament to national resolve. About being united in purpose to forge a brighter dawn, and each tap of the keys felt like driving another nail into his own coffin. He saved the draft and sent it on for distribution. The deed done and the lie disseminated, and then he closed the terminal window and watched the screen go dark, reflecting back his own tired and ashen stained face.

He opened the drawer again to look at his daughter's unopened letters. Knowing he could not answer them with truth. Knowing that any answer without truth would only endanger her further. His silence was a shield, a coward's shield, he knew it and she knew it. The scrap in his pocket pressed against his thigh like a persistent and tiny ache. A reminder of a different kind of truth that was buried but not gone. He pulled out a blank sheet of pulp paper and picked up a pen. His hand hovering over the page as he considered what he could possibly write that would not be a lie and would not bring danger. No words came to him that could erase the image she had of him as a propagandist, a liar and a burner of truth.

He put the pen down, folded the blank paper and slipped it back into the drawer, another silence added to the growing pile. The scrap in his pocket felt heavier now. The accusation "...*WAS LIAR...*" now seeming to be about him in the present moment and not some unknown figure from the ashes. The shift bell clanged its harsh and metallic signal to end the day. Elias stood up with protesting joints, gathering nothing but himself as he walked out past the silent desks, down the echoing stairwell and through the lobby. There a bleached image of the Leader watched from a framed poster by the door. His smile blurred and his eyes empty.

Outside, the cold evening air hit him with the force of a relief. He began to walk without any destination in mind, not towards home but simply away. He walked past the trampled leaflets and the faded posters and all the hieroglyphs of decay that Mira also saw. He walked until he reached the wide, gray and slow-moving river where oily rainbows shimmered on its surface near the outflow pipes. He stood on the bank and looked at the dark water. Thinking of the furnace and the ash it produced and the words that were destroyed. Thinking of his daughter's letters burning in their own way, and thinking of the fragile and charred truth in his pocket.

He reached into his pocket and pulled out the folded scrap and unfolded it. The paper now soft and worn. The words still painfully clear. A gust of wind snatched at the paper and pulled it from his fingers before he could react. It fluttered and twisted in the air before diving towards the greasy water. He lunged for it but his fingers brushed only empty air. The scrap landed on the dark surface and floated for a single second with the words "...*WAS LIAR*..." facing the sky before the water soaked through and the paper darkened and sank. It vanished completely beneath the slow and uncaring current.

It was gone. Like the volumes in the furnace and like the missing boy and like the taken man and like truth itself. Swallowed by the gray water without a trace. He stared at the spot where it had disappeared until the ripples faded away, the river flowing on in its silent and indifferent way. He stood there empty-handed as the wind cut through his coat and the sour taste of the pressroom returned to his mouth. Then he turned away from the water to start the long walk home. His pocket feeling lighter and emptier but the accusation now etched not on paper but on the inside of his own skull. He walked past the now empty and cleaned Victory Plaza with its cold braziers. He saw Mira's face in his mind as she knelt to sweep ash into her jar, holding absence in a tangible form. He touched his own empty pocket and knew he had no jar. Only the stain of soot on his hands, the echo of burning and the ghost of words now drowned in the river.

The walk home was a trudge through a city that felt increasingly alien to him. He turned down his own street where the apartment building looked like all the others, gray and crumbling. He saw the light on in his third-floor window where his wife would be preparing their meager rations, living within the silence he maintained for their safety. He paused at the entrance and looked up at the window, a knot tightening in his stomach. The silence inside was not just an absence of sound but the space where his daughter's accusations lived and where his wife's quiet disappointment resided and where the words he burned echoed the loudest. He took a breath of the cold air that hurt his lungs and reached for the door handle. His gaze snagged on a fresh notice taped to the wall beside the entrance, slightly crooked on its crisp paper with bold black type. A new directive from Precinct Command that he had not seen that morning. He stepped closer to read the short and brutal words, his blood slowing and the cold seeping past his skin into his bones as the implications unfolded with a cold and precise logic. Another layer of silence and another brick in the wall. He looked up again at his lit window where his wife moved behind the glass, oblivious to the new words and the new silence they demanded. The door handle felt colder than ice. He released the handle and walked away, down the street. He needed air, he needed anything but the silence he knew was waiting for him.

He usually took the most direct route, but tonight his feet carried him on a detour. Drawn by a sound that was the antithesis of the sterile silence of the pressroom and the roaring void of the furnace. It was the sound of a saxophone, raw and soulful, bleeding from the basement vent of a nondescript building. A small, unlit sign simply read "The Jazz Club."

This was a place of tolerated heresy. The regime allowed it to exist, perhaps believing it was a useful outlet, a pressure valve for the artistic and intellectual energies it could not entirely extinguish. Or perhaps they simply didn't understand it. The music that came from here was complex, improvisational, and deeply emotional—everything the regime's rigid, pre-composed marches were not. It spoke of individual expression, of pain and joy that were personal, not state-sanctioned.

Elias stood in the shadows across the street, listening. The door opened briefly as someone left. A wave of warm, complex sound washed over him—the wail of the sax, the thump of a bass, the shimmer of a cymbal. It was a language of truth. For a moment, he was not the man who burned the past; he was just a man, moved by a beautiful, sad noise. He thought of the scrap of paper in the river. *Liar and thief.* The music felt like an answer to that accusation, a proof that some truths could not be burned or drowned.

But he couldn't go in. To be seen there was a risk. More than that, he felt unworthy. The musicians in there were brave, speaking in a code the regime couldn't break. He, who set fire to words for a living, had no right to share their air. The door closed, and the sound faded back to a muffled throb. The spell was broken. The guilt returned, sharper now, amplified by the beauty he had just witnessed but was too cowardly to embrace.

He turned away and continued his walk, the knot in his stomach tightening. He passed the monolithic structure of the *Bureau of Counter Intelligence*. Its windows were dark, but Elias felt a familiar dread looking at it. This was where his daughter's education was being "guided." The BCI opposed intelligence the way a weed killer opposed life. Its purpose was to sterilize young minds, to ensure they never asked a dangerous question or formed an original thought. He imagined the classrooms inside: lessons on the Leader's infallibility, mathematics problems calculating production quotas that didn't exist, history classes that were just recitations of bulletins from the Hall of Historical Corrections. He had helped write those bulletins. He was complicit in poisoning his own daughter's mind.

His feet carried him faster now, a desperate urge to get home, to shut the door on the world. But the city had one more landmark to confront him with. On the corner, a grand old building of science, once a university laboratory, stood behind a high fence. A new sign, illuminated by a single, stark spotlight, declared it *The Institution of Heretical Science*. This was the Leader's masterstroke. The nation's brightest minds, those who insisted on following evidence and reason, had been gathered here not to be celebrated, but to be quarantined and demonized. Their peer-reviewed papers were labeled "heretical texts." Their experiments were called "reckless apostasy against the national spirit." The regime couldn't dismantle the laws of physics, so it instead mocked and pathologized those who understood them. Elias looked up at the darkened windows. Were they in there now, those heretics? Were they still running experiments, still seeking truth, even when their government had officially declared it a thought-crime? Their stubbornness made his own compliance feel even more vile.

He finally returned to his apartment building. The notice on the door he had seen earlier was a directive from the *Bureau of Belligerent Blunder Heads*. It was, typically, a masterpiece of idiocy. It announced a new, mandatory "Neighborhood Harmony" initiative, requiring all residents to report weekly on "acts of communal goodwill" performed by their neighbors. It was a scheme designed to turn everyone into a spy, to create a culture of performative loyalty and snitching. It had the Bureau's fingerprints all over it: belligerent in its intrusion, a blunder in its clumsy obviousness, and utterlyheaded in its execution. It was the kind of policy that only made sense in the halls of power, where sycophants competed to present the Leader with the most ludicrously loyal ideas.

Elias pushed the door open and stepped into the hallway, the notice burning in his mind. He climbed the stairs, each step heavier than the last. He wasn't just carrying the soot from the furnace anymore. He was carrying the sound from the Jazz Club, the shame of the BCI, the grim defiance of the Heretical Scientists, and the stupid, crushing weight of the Blunder Heads' latest decree. He was a walking archive of the nation's schizophrenia. And waiting for him at the top was the silence of his apartment, a silence he had chosen, a silence that was now the loudest sound of all.

Chapter 4

The small bathroom was filled with a profound and heavy silence that pressed against his ears. He turned the simple lock on the door with a soft and final click. A necessary part of the ritual he had performed too many times before. From the inner pocket of his worn jacket he removed a single sheet of paper, a letter he had written over the course of several days filled with hollow excuses and weak explanations for his own profound failings. He would never send this particular letter to his daughter for he understood its contents were just another layer of the same pervasive dishonesty that defined his life now. The act of writing it was a pathetic attempt to soothe his own conscience, and the act of destroying it was the only honest part of the entire process.

He struck a single match against the rough side of the matchbox, and the sudden flare of light illuminated his tired face in the dimness of the small room. The sharp and familiar scent of sulfur bloomed in the air around him for a brief and pungent moment. He held the small flame to the bottom corner of the paper and watched with a detached fascination as the fire began its slow and hungry consumption of his own inadequate words. The edges of the page blackened and curled inward, transforming the carefully constructed sentences into fragile and weightless carbon.

He held the burning page over the white porcelain of the bathroom sink, his fingers feeling the growing heat of the approaching flames. He allowed the final fragment to fall from his grasp into the dry basin where it crumbled into a small pile of fine gray ash. He turned the tap and let a stream of cold water wash the remains of his confession down the metal drain, erasing the physical evidence of his weakness. He washed his hands thoroughly with a plain bar of soap, scrubbing at his skin as if he could remove more than just the smell of smoke. His own reflection in the mirror above the sink showed him a man he barely recognized anymore, a man who performed these dismal chores of moral compromise.

He unlocked the door and stepped back out into the hallway of the apartment, the faint and acrid smell of smoke following him like a guilty spirit. His wife was already in the small kitchen setting the table for their evening meal with a quiet and efficient economy of movement. She placed two plain plates and two water glasses upon the worn surface of the table without making a sound. She did not lift her eyes to meet his own because she had heard the strike of the match and had smelled the results of its small fire. This was their well-established routine, a silent understanding of the things they would never discuss aloud.

They sat down together at the table to eat their meal in a silence that felt as heavy as stone. The food upon their plates was simple and bland, a meal of boiled potatoes and a single slice of dark bread for each of them. There was no meat to be found on the table because meat had become a distant memory from another time entirely. They ate without speaking to one another, and the only sound in the room was the quiet scraping of their metal forks against the ceramic plates.

He tried to think of something ordinary to say about the mundane events of his day at the office. He thought about the immense heat of the basement furnace and the important looking documents he had fed into its flames. He thought about the scrap of paper he had saved from the fire and the strange words written upon it. He thought about the cold wind coming off the river as he walked home. He said absolutely nothing about any of these things because they were not subjects for polite dinner conversation in this apartment.

His wife kept her eyes fixed upon her own plate of food, her thin hands resting in her lap beneath the table. She was not really eating her meal so much as she was waiting for the uncomfortable silence of the dinner to reach its natural conclusion. A sudden noise from the hallway beyond the kitchen made them both look up from their food at the very same time. It was the distinct sound of a key turning with some difficulty in the lock of their front door.

The heavy wooden door swung inward and bumped against the wall behind it. They heard the sound of a heavy bag being dropped onto the floor of the entryway. Then their daughter, Jenna was suddenly there in the kitchen doorway. Standing with her coat still on and her hair messy from the wind. She was supposed to be away at her college classes miles and miles from this apartment. She stood before them with her shoulders slumped forward in a posture of pure exhaustion, a large duffel bag resting against her feet on the floor.

Her face was terribly pale and her eyes were dark hollows in her head. She looked much older than her years and immeasurably tired down to her very soul. Her mother stood up from the table so quickly that her wooden chair scraped loudly against the floor tiles. She asked what was wrong and why she'd come home without any warning. Jenna didn't even glance in her mother's direction. She kept her flat and cold gaze fixed directly upon him.

She told them in a hoarse and drained voice that the school administration had sent her home. She said the word expelled into the quiet room and let it hang there in the air between them. It was such a final and decisive word. A word that closed every door to a future. He asked her why this terrible thing had happened, and the word itself was dry and painful in his own throat. She gave a bitter and twisted imitation of a smile then and said the official reason was seditionist revisionism.

She explained that she had asked a simple question during her history class about the official reports of the last harvest and the widespread famine that followed it. Her teacher had reported the question to the administration office immediately, and the judgment had been swift and absolute. His wife brought a hand up to cover her mouth, and her eyes grew wide with a familiar and deep-seated fear. Expulsion from college was a serious matter on its own, but the official reason given was infinitely more dangerous for the entire family.

Jenna took another step further into the kitchen without breaking her cold stare in his direction. She reached into the pocket of her heavy coat and pulled out a small notebook with a plain cardboard cover. She said they had allowed her to pack her own belongings under close supervision before leaving the campus. She said they had either not seen the notebook or simply had not cared enough to confiscate it from her. She held the small book out toward him, bypassing her mother completely, and placed it directly into his waiting hands.

She told him it was for him alone to read and to keep. She said she had written something inside it before any of this trouble had started, and she felt he should be the one to see it now. She did not wait for him to open the cover or to offer any response to her statement. She simply picked her heavy bag up from the floor and walked down the short hallway to her old childhood bedroom. She closed the door behind herself and turned the lock with a quiet and definitive click.

His wife remained frozen in her place by the table, one hand still pressed against her mouth. She stared for a long moment at the closed door of Jenna's room. Then she turned her head slowly and looked at the plain notebook held in his hand. She looked directly into his face as if searching for some answer he could not possibly give her. Without saying a single word, she turned back toward the kitchen sink and picked up a dirty plate from the counter. She began to wash the plate with a frantic and focused intensity, her shoulders shaking with the force of her silent crying.

He stood alone in the middle of the kitchen for a long time holding the notebook. He walked finally into the living room and sat down heavily in his own worn armchair. The light in the room was low and cast long shadows across the floor. He opened the cover of the small notebook and looked at the first page. All the other pages in the book were completely blank and untouched. There was only a single line of writing in his daughter's neat and precise handwriting.

He read the line once and then he read it again, but the words remained exactly the same. They were simple and direct and absolutely devastating in their implication. He closed the cover of the notebook and placed it on the small table beside his chair, next to a lamp with a cracked shade. He could still hear the sound of running water from the kitchen sink and the soft and muffled sounds of his wife's crying.

He went to the cupboard in the corner of the room and took out a bottle of cheap alcohol. He poured a full glass of the clear liquid and drank it down in one long burning swallow. It burned its way down his throat and spread a false warmth through his chest. He drank another glass and then another until the sharp edges of the room began to soften and blur into something more manageable. But the words from the notebook remained perfectly clear and sharp in his mind, entirely unaffected by the alcohol.

He looked across the room at the small and plain notebook resting on the table. It was just a simple object made of paper and cardboard, an ordinary thing. But it felt as heavy as a block of solid lead, a weight that would never lift from his shoulders. *The truth is a widow*, he thought to himself, and *it always outlives her eulogies*. He poured himself another full glass of the cheap alcohol and drank it down. The room continued to soften around its edges, but the words remained, hard and clear and permanent.

The cheap alcohol did nothing to drown the memory of his daughter's face, or the chilling bureaucratic term she had used: *seditionist revisionism*. It was a phrase straight from the **Bureau of Counter Intelligence**'s official lexicon. The BCI didn't just teach falsehoods; it policed the very boundaries of thought. Her crime wasn't just asking a question; it was attempting to "revise" state-approved reality. Elias knew the process. Her teacher, a party loyalist vetted by the BCI, would have filed an "Ideological Deviation Report" within hours. The college's administration, terrified of losing their funding or worse, would have held a sham disciplinary hearing. There would be no defense, no appeal. The system was designed to be a swift, brutal conveyor belt from classroom to blacklist.

He thought of the campus now, not as a place of learning, but as a factory for ideological conformity. The BCI's influence would be everywhere. The humanities departments would be eviscerated, their libraries replaced with a single, approved bookshelf curated by the Bureau. Science classes would be taught from textbooks published by the *Institution of Heretical Science*—not the real, groundbreaking work the Institution's scientists had once done, but bowdlerized, simplified pamphlets that twisted real concepts into propaganda. Physics lessons would be about the "irrefutable force of the Leader's will," biology about the "purity of the national body." His daughter, with her sharp mind and hunger for real knowledge, would have been a walking provocation in such a place.

He poured another glass, his hand trembling. The notebook on the table seemed to pulse with a dark energy. He knew what was inside. He had seen the look in her eyes—not just anger, but a profound, disillusioned pity. *For him.* He was the one who wrote the words that filled the BCI's textbooks. He was the one who composed the glowing editorials about the "educational triumphs" of the regime, praising the very system that had just broken his child.

The sound of his wife's weeping from the kitchen had subsided into a hollow silence. He imagined her at the sink, staring out the window at the darkening city. Her world shrunk to this apartment, this fear, this crushing disappointment. Her life's work had been raising their daughter, protecting her, hoping for a future brighter than their present. And in one day, that future had been extinguished by a faceless bureaucracy he served.

A new, more terrifying thought occurred to him. Expulsion was not the end. It was the beginning. Her name would now be on a list. She would be unpersoned. No other school would take her. She would be ineligible for any job above manual labor. She would be a subject of interest for the Order Compliance Bureau, the same people who had taken Tomasz Varga. Their knock on the door was not a matter of *if,* but *when.* And he, Elias, with his access and his position, was powerless to stop it. His complicity had bought them nothing but a slower descent.

He lurched out of his chair, the room swaying. He couldn't sit with this knowledge. He had to move, to walk, to outpace the dread. He stumbled out of the apartment, down the stairs, and into the cold night air, leaving his wife with her silence and his daughter behind her locked door.

He walked without direction, his feet carrying him on a path of familiar misery. He found himself standing before the great, dark edifice of the central *Library of Errors*. It was closed, its massive doors chained. But a single light burned in an upstairs office—some librarian-turned-censor, working late to ensure the next day's "curated" selection of books perfectly aligned with the latest directives from the Hall of Historical Corrections.

This was the endpoint of his career. This was where all his burned archives and polished lies were meant to lead: a world with only one book, one story, one voice. A world where his daughter's question was a thought-crime, and her notebook was a dangerous, heretical text. He pressed his forehead against the cold stone of the library's wall. He was an architect of this silence, a bricklayer for this prison of the mind.

The words from the notebook echoed in his head, a relentless, sober mantra beneath the fog of alcohol. He had read them only once, but they were etched onto the back of his eyes.

"The truth is a widow who outlives her eulogies."

His daughter hadn't just written an accusation. She had written a prophecy. He could burn every document in the city. He could write a thousand lies. He could stand by and let them dismantle education and silence music and lock away the heretical scientists. But it wouldn't matter. The truth didn't need him. It would persist, a widow in mourning clothes, waiting patiently for all those who tried to bury her to die off first. And she would outlive them. She would outlive *him*.

He pushed himself away from the wall and turned toward home, the alcohol now a sour sickness in his gut. The silence that awaited him there was no longer just the absence of sound. It was the presence of that widow, sitting in his armchair, holding his daughter's notebook, waiting for him to finally speak a word that was true.

Chapter 5

The Cathedral of Progress stood as a stark and imposing silhouette against the flat gray expanse of the sky. A structure that did not invite prayer but rather demanded a cold and silent awe from all who looked upon it. Its lines were severe and its angles were sharp, a monument to a new kind of faith built from steel and unforgiving glass instead of wood and stone. A single needle-like spire pierced the low clouds, a deliberate threat aimed at heaven itself. The walls below were smooth and utterly blank, devoid of any ornamentation that might suggest warmth or history. The only source of color on the entire vast façade was the enormous round window placed high above the main entrance, a massive stained-glass representation of a single human eye that stared out with unblinking intensity over the entire city square. This was the Leader's own eye rendered in countless fragments of colored glass, and its gaze was inescapable for every person gathered below.

A great crowd had assembled within the square, a sea of people standing shoulder to shoulder in the cold air, all of them perfectly silent and unnaturally still. Their collective faces were turned upward toward the high platform erected before the Cathedral's immense sealed doors. Their expressions were uniformly blank, a carefully maintained mask of dutiful attention. Mira stood somewhere within the center of this press of bodies, feeling the heat of strangers on either side of her while a deep chill seemed to radiate from the stone walls of the new building. She kept her own eyes lowered, refusing to look directly into the great glass eye above. Instead she studied the people around her, searching their faces for any sign of the unease she felt herself.

The logistics of the event were a masterpiece of controlled chaos, orchestrated by the *Bureau of Belligerent Blunder Heads*. Their incompetence was legendary in matters of statecraft, but they excelled at stagecraft and security. Bull-necked men in ill-fitting suits. Their faces flushed with self-importance, scurried around the perimeter, barking contradictory orders into their wrist radios. They were the perfect choice for this: their belligerence cowed the crowd, and their blunder-headed nature meant they followed orders without the inconvenient spark of doubt that might afflict a more intelligent person. They had cordoned off the square with brutal efficiency. Their presence a reminder that this consecration was not an invitation but a command performance. One of them, his chest puffed out, was berating a junior officer for a microscopic scuff on his boot, utterly oblivious to the profound unease of the thousands he was meant to be controlling. It was a perfect metaphor for the regime: obsessed with surface-level perfection while the foundations rotted.

The Leader himself was already standing upon the platform. A figure of profound and unsettling stillness amidst the anticipation of the crowd. He was dressed in a simple and unadorned black suit that seemed to absorb the weak afternoon light. His hands hung relaxed at his sides, making no gesture toward the people who watched him. He did not need to shout or move to hold their complete attention. His mere presence on the platform was enough to command a total and absolute silence that felt heavier than any noise. He simply stood there and allowed the crowd to wait upon his first word, demonstrating that his power was not something he needed to exert but simply something that existed.

A choir of young boys was arranged in neat rows on a smaller platform off to one side, each of them dressed in identical robes of brilliant white that looked too thin for the cold weather. Their faces had been scrubbed clean and their hair had been cut short in a uniform style. They stared straight ahead with blank expressions. They began to sing a hymn without any signal that Mira could see. Their high clear voices rising together in practiced harmony to fill the entire square with sound. The words of the hymn were about national strength and the virtue of absolute unity. A simple and repetitive melody designed to be easily remembered and recited.

Mira found herself watching the boys as they sang, her eyes moving from one young face to another until her attention settled on a single boy near the back of the group. His mouth was open and the correct sounds were emerging, but the movement of his lips was a half-beat behind the movements of all the other boys around him. His eyes were not fixed upon the Leader or upon some distant point of focus like the others, but were instead scanning the crowd below with a look of naked fear. He was singing the words of strength and unity, but his entire body seemed to tell a different and more anxious story.

The song rose toward its final and most powerful chord, and every boy in the choir held the last note with a precision that must have required weeks of rehearsal. As the sustained note finally ended, the boy with the unsynchronized lips brought his hands together in a single clap that was lost within the greater sound of the crowd's applause. It was a small and seemingly natural movement, but the motion caused the cuff of his white robe to pull back for just a second from his wrist. Mira saw a few letters stitched into the hidden inner lining of the cuff with a thread of vivid red. A single word that was there and gone again in a flash before the cuff fell back into place and the boy dropped his hands to his sides. The word was *remember*.

A perfect silence fell over the square once more as the Leader took a single step forward on the platform. His calm voice carrying to every corner of the open space without any apparent effort. He said this new building was not a structure made from stone and glass but was instead a building made from pure human will. A solid manifestation of their collective resolve and his own singular vision. He said this was the place where they would all come to worship the idea of progress itself. A place where they would finally become one single people with one single eye and one single voice and one single purpose for the future.

His voice was a hypnotic drone, a weaponized monotony that sought to lull the mind into submission. He spoke of purity, of a future scrubbed clean of the messy complexities of the past. But his words were subtly undermined by another sound, a ghost at the edge of hearing. From across the city, the *Tower of Song* continued its eternal broadcast. Today, the song was a mournful, ancient folk melody, a tune of loss and longing that predated the regime, the Leader, and the very concept of the nation itself. It wove through the gaps in his speech, a haunting counterpoint to his rhetoric of unity. *"We are one people,"* he said. The Tower's song spoke of individual sorrow, of a soul's lonely journey. *"We have a single purpose,"* he insisted. The melody spoke of a thousand different paths and a million private dreams. The crowd seemed to feel the dissonance; a slight restlessness stirred within them. A collective, unconscious leaning toward the Tower's more honest music. The Leader's eye twitched, almost imperceptibly. He could rename plazas and burn books, but he could not silence the Tower. Its persistence was a quiet humiliation, a reminder that some forms of beauty were beyond his control.

He spoke for some time about the necessity of strength and the absolute importance of purity in thought and action. He said the past was a sickness that had infected the nation for generations, and this new Cathedral standing behind him was the only possible cure for that long illness. An old woman with a narrow face was standing very close to Mira, her thin hands clutching a worn shawl around her shoulders. The woman leaned toward Mira without turning her head, and her voice was the softest possible whisper meant for Mira's ears alone.

She said they had come for her neighbor just last week. A man who had played his radio too loud and who had often sung old songs from a time before the current government. She said she had told the man who collected the rents about the noise, and that man had given her extra rations for the information. A bag of sugar and a full can of meat. She swallowed with some difficulty and said they had taken her neighbor away for a period of correction, and now his apartment was perfectly quiet. The woman's eyes were strangely bright as she spoke, and Mira could see a mixture of pride and shame in her expression that seemed to have merged into a single unnameable emotion. The woman said the sugar had been very sweet before she turned away and disappeared completely into the moving crowd.

On the opposite side of the great square, Elias stood near the press reporters, holding an official notebook and a pen he had been given for his work. He was meant to record the events of the consecration for the newspaper, but his head was pounding and the light reflecting off the Cathedral's glass eye was too bright for his eyes. His mouth held the stale taste of cheap alcohol from the night before, and his mind repeated his daughter's words like a desperate mantra. *The truth is a widow who outlives her eulogies.*

He wrote down the Leader's words in a hurried shorthand, knowing they were the same empty words that were always spoken, the same hollow promises of strength and unity and progress. He looked past the Leader at the cold façade of the Cathedral, and he saw the crew of workmen still standing on their scaffolding, ready to clear away the last of their tools now that the ceremony was ending. One of the men was leaning heavily against a safety rail, his body slumped with a deep exhaustion that Elias could feel even from a distance. The worker looked out over the crowd for a moment. His eyes met the eyes of Elias across the space between them.

For a single second, a look of perfect understanding passed between the two men. A silent recognition of the shared wrongness of the spectacle they were witnessing. A mutual acknowledgment of the great lie they were both helping to maintain. Then the worker quickly looked down at his boots, and the moment of connection was broken as if it had never happened. The Leader finished his speech with a raised hand that was both a blessing and a dismissal, and the crowd began to move all at once, turning away from the Cathedral and starting the process of dispersal.

High above on the choir platform, the boys in white robes were filing down a narrow set of stairs to rejoin their handlers. The boy with the red thread stitched into his cuff was the last to leave, and as he passed by a piece of sharp metal on the scaffolding, his sleeve caught on the edge and pulled tight. A single long red thread unraveled from the cuff and was pulled free from the white fabric, catching the wind immediately. It lifted into the air above the crowd, a thin red line dancing against the dull gray sky, and it floated higher and higher until it caught for just a moment on the very tip of the golden spire. Then the wind took hold of it once more, pulling it free and carrying it away over the rooftops of the city toward some unknown street or some unseen crack where it might finally come to rest.

As the crowd dissolved into a river of gray coats flowing out of the square, Mira didn't move. She watched the red thread until it vanished from sight, a tiny, defiant spark against the monochrome sky. It felt like a message, a thread of memory cast adrift for someone to find. Then, her eyes were drawn downward. There, on the pristine new curbstone, was a fresh mark. It was the same symbol she'd seen near the drainpipe days before: the small, etched wave of *The Undercurrent*. It had been scratched there during the ceremony, right under the noses of the Blunder Heads. Her heart quickened. They were here. They had witnessed this too. The mark wasn't just a signal; it was a dare. *We see what you see.*

Elias, meanwhile, walked as if in a trance. The brief, silent connection with the worker had shattered something inside him. He wasn't alone in his complicity. There were others, trapped in the same machine, who also saw the cracks. The weight of the **Cathedral of Progress** behind him felt immense, not as a symbol of strength, but as a tombstone. It was a mausoleum for truth, a monument to a single, monstrous ego. Its silence wasn't peaceful; it was the silence of a vacuum, sucking all other sounds—dissent, doubt, conversation, even the echo of the Tower of Song—into its void. He thought of the **Cathedral of Silence** across the city, its terrifying acoustic properties used to break wills. This new cathedral was its ideological twin: a place designed to stifle not sound, but soul.

He knew his article for the *Beacon* would have to be a masterpiece of obfuscation. He would write of the Leader's "vision" and the people's "fervent devotion." He would describe the Cathedral as a "beacon of hope." The words were already writing themselves in his mind, each one a betrayal of the worker's haunted eyes, a betrayal of his daughter, a betrayal of the red thread. The truth was a widow, and he was once again officiating at her funeral.

Mira finally turned to leave, the cold seeping through her coat. The consecration was over, but the Cathedral's work had just begun. It would stand there for a thousand years, its glass eye staring. A permanent claim on the city's skyline and its psyche. But as she walked away, she held onto the images the Leader had not intended: the boy's fear, the red thread, the worker's exhaustion, the tiny etched wave on the curb. These were the real consecration. Not of glass and steel, but of resolve. The Cathedral was meant to be the end of the story. But for Mira, and for Elias, and for the unknown hand that had etched the symbol, it felt like the beginning.

Part II

Chapter 1

The air within the repurposed basement of the derelict button factory was thick and heavy with the accumulated breath of its secret occupants. A damp atmosphere that carried the lingering scent of wet brick and the faint metallic tang of old machine oil. A single string of bare electric bulbs hung from the low ceiling on frayed wires. Casting a weak and yellowish light that pooled on the uneven concrete floor and left the distant corners of the large room in deep and concealing shadow. People sat crowded together upon wooden crates and overturned storage boxes. Their bodies perfectly still and their faces all turned toward the center of the room where a woman stood waiting in the dim light. Her name was Rosa, and she had a small wooden table placed before her with twelve simple water glasses arranged in a neat row upon its surface. Each glass had been filled to a different level with water from a metal jug, creating a set of potential instruments for the evening's performance.

She did not look out at the expectant faces of the crowd gathered around her, keeping her complete focus instead upon the twelve glasses waiting on the table. She dipped the tips of her fingers into a small ceramic bowl of water that she kept beside the jug, shaking off the excess moisture with a practiced flick of her wrist. She began to run her wet finger slowly around the rim of the very first glass, applying a steady and even pressure to the smooth surface. A single clear note bloomed into the silence of the basement, a pure and resonant tone that hung in the air for a long moment before slowly fading away. She moved her hand to the next glass in the sequence and produced another note, this one slightly lower in pitch than the first one had been.

The sounds she produced did not form any kind of recognizable melody or song that anyone could name. Instead, it followed a very specific and deliberate pattern of short and long tones. The rhythm of the notes felt familiar to several of the older people in the room. A pattern that spoke of an old language almost forgotten. A language built from clicks and pauses and silent spaces between sounds. She played the exact same sequence of notes three separate times without any variation, a short note followed by a long note and then another short one, then a pause, then two long notes in a row, another pause, and finally a long note, a short note, and a long note to finish.

Some of the people in the audience closed their eyes as they listened to the ethereal music, concentrating on the pattern of sounds and translating the notes into letters within their own minds. The letters slowly formed themselves into a single powerful word that echoed inside their heads. The word was *remember*. She was tapping out a message for them using only water and glass, a word of defiance and a call to memory in a time of enforced forgetting. She finished the sequence for the final time and let the last clear note fade completely into the quiet of the basement room. The only sound that remained was the distant and rhythmic drip of water from a leaking pipe somewhere in the darkness behind them. For a single moment, there was a perfect and profound peace within that hidden space.

Then the heavy wooden door at the top of the stairs exploded inward with a violent and splintering crash that shattered the silence completely. There was no warning knock or demand for entry, only the sudden destruction of the door as it broke apart under the force of several heavy boots. Bright white light from the street outside came flooding down the stairs into the dark basement, illuminating the shocked faces of the people sitting there. Several tall figures stood silhouetted in the broken doorway. Their features hidden by the glare of the light behind them but their gray uniforms clearly visible. They moved down the stairs with a fast and brutal efficiency, fanning out into the room without speaking a single word to anyone present.

The people in the audience rose to their feet as one body, the sound of scraping crates and boxes filling the air now instead of music. There was no screaming or shouting from the crowd, only a sharp and collective intake of breath that seemed to suck all the air from the room. One of the gray-uniformed guards walked directly over to Rosa's table and looked down at the row of water glasses with an expression of cold curiosity. He picked up one of the glasses and examined it for a second as if it were some kind of strange and dangerous insect. Then he simply opened his hand and let the glass fall to the concrete floor where it exploded into a thousand pieces, water and glass shards spreading out in a wide circle around his boots.

He picked up another glass and dropped it as well, then another and another until he had methodically destroyed every single one of the twelve glasses on the table. The sharp wet popping sounds of breaking glass filled the entire room, and the smell of spilled water began to mix with the dust in the air. Another guard walked over to a shadowy corner of the basement where a trumpet case had been left leaning against the wall. He stomped down on the case with his heavy boot until the metal buckled and broke, then he picked up a clarinet from a nearby chair and snapped the wooden instrument over his knee with a dry cracking sound. They were systematically erasing all the sound from the room, breaking every object that could possibly be used to make music or send messages.

The guards began motioning for the people to leave the basement immediately, pointing toward the broken doorway with impersonal gestures. The crowd started to move slowly toward the stairs, filing out into the cold night air outside without looking back at the destruction left behind. Rosa remained standing beside her ruined table. Her hands hanging at her sides as she looked down at the shards of glass and the water soaking into the dirt floor. The guard who had broken her glasses stood in front of her and pointed toward the door, but she didn't move or acknowledge his command in any way.

The guard took a single step closer to her and raised his hand, not to strike her but to push her physically toward the exit. Then a new sound started somewhere at the back of the room, a low and steady humming noise that seemed to vibrate through the air itself. A man with his eyes closed was humming a single sustained note, the exact same note that the first water glass had produced for the letter 'R'. Another person joined him in the humming. A woman with her hands clasped together, and then another person added their voice to the sound. The humming grew louder and more powerful, becoming a deep resonant frequency that filled the entire basement and seemed to shake the very walls around them.

It was a sound they were making with their own bodies. A sound that could not be confiscated or broken or left behind on the floor. The guard stopped his advance toward Rosa and turned his head toward the source of the humming. His face showing clear confusion about how to stop this kind of resistance. The hum continued to grow in volume and power. A wordless but defiant sound that carried the same message the glasses had carried. A message they would now carry within themselves out into the night. The guard lowered his hand and took a step back from Rosa, looking at her face one last time before turning to walk out of the basement with the other guards following behind him.

They left the broken door and the silence they had created, but the hum did not stop with their departure. It continued to fill the empty space of the basement, a promise made of sound and breath. The club was gone and the instruments were broken, but the hum remained inside each person as they walked away in different directions through the dark streets. The sound was quiet now and under the breath, but it was still there as a current running through the entire city. A word passed from one person to another without speaking. A sound that could not be caught or contained. It was just a simple hum, but it felt like a true beginning of something larger. The guard's badge had the number 8647 stamped into its metal surface, and that same number was painted on the side of a broken crate near the door, a number that would appear again and again throughout the city in the days to come, a number on a piece of fading graffiti on a wall that people would see and remember.

The cold night air was a shock after the close, charged atmosphere of the basement. The attendees scattered quickly, melting into the labyrinth of alleys around the button factory, each carrying the hum inside them like a secret ember. Rosa was one of the last to leave, stepping over the splintered remains of the door. She didn't look back. The place was ruined, a sanctuary violated. But as she walked, the hum persisted, not just in her memory, but in the air around her. From a nearby alley, she heard it—a low, sustained note from a man in the shadows. A woman passing on the other side of the street echoed it, just for a second, before turning a corner. It was alive. It was spreading.

This was no longer just a gathering of disaffected individuals. The raid had forged them into something else. The shared experience of the broken glasses, the shattered instruments, and the collective hum had been a baptism. They now had a shared language, a shared symbol, and a shared enemy. The amorphous feeling of resistance had crystallized into a network. They needed a name. The word came to Rosa as she walked, given form by the secret, flowing nature of their communication. They were **The Undercurrent**. They were the hidden flow beneath the stagnant surface of the regime. They were persistent, quiet, strong. Their power lay in their invisibility, in the regime's inability to grasp something that had no leader, no headquarters, and no manifesto beyond a single, hummed word: *remember*.

Mira heard about the raid the next day. The news traveled not through official channels, which were silent, but through the new, fragile web of whispers. At the water queue, a woman ahead of her turned and murmured, "They broke the music last night. Near the old factory." The woman's eyes held a new, hard light. "But they couldn't break the tune." Mira felt a jolt of fear, followed by a surge of fierce pride. Lena's husband, Tomasz, had been a regular at those basement gatherings. This was his world, and now it was hers. The blood on her November jar felt like a direct link to this new defiance.

Elias, at his desk at the *Beacon*, was given a tersely worded memo to type up for the next edition. It was a triumphantly short piece, declaring that a "seditionist meeting hall" used for "anti-progress ideological trafficking" had been shut down by vigilant authorities. The memo, he knew, had originated from the *Bureau of Belligerent Blunder Heads*, taking credit for an operation they'd likely bungled until a more competent security branch had to step in. He typed the lies, his fingers feeling numb. *Seditionist meeting hall*. It had been a room where people made music. *Ideological trafficking*. They had been sharing a memory. Each word he typed was a betrayal of the hum he now carried in his own heart, a hum he'd heard echoing from the *Tower of Song* that very morning, as if the Tower itself was acknowledging the new, human counterpoint to its eternal melody.

That night, in a dozen apartments across the city, the hum was passed on. A father hummed it to his young child as a lullaby. A tune whose meaning the child would feel before he could understand it. A group of workers hummed it softly as they repaired a road, their breath steaming in the cold air, their shared sound a bond the foreman could not perceive. The guard who had been at the raid, ID# 8647, filed his report, calling it a "successful dispersal of a public nuisance." But in the quiet of his own barracks that night, he found the simple, haunting sequence of notes running through his head on an endless loop. He couldn't remember why he had been so determined to silence it.

The Undercurrent had no center. It was everywhere and nowhere. Its headquarters were *The Jazz Club* back room, where the owner, a man with sad eyes and nimble fingers, now offered a safe haven and a knowing nod to those who mentioned the "water music."

Its archives were the memories of its people, and its library was the city itself, where the symbol of the wave began to appear—scratched into a park bench, chalked onto a wall, stitched into the hem of a coat. They had been scattered, but they had been seeded. The regime had tried to silence a sound and had instead given it a thousand new mouths. The hum was the heartbeat of the resistance now, quiet, steady, and impossible to stop.

Chapter 2

The silence within Rosa's small apartment felt heavier and more profound than it ever had before, a tangible presence that seemed to press against the thin walls and the single window overlooking the street. Her mother stood motionless by that window, holding an old winter coat made of heavy wool that was far too warm for the current season, her fingers tracing the worn fabric with a strange and distant reverence. She asked Rosa to bring her the seam ripper from the sewing box on the shelf, her voice so soft it was almost a whisper in the quiet room. Rosa found the small metal tool with its sharp and delicate point. She handed it to her mother without asking any questions about what she intended to do with it. Her mother moved to her favorite chair by the cold fireplace and turned the heavy coat completely inside out with a practiced efficiency.

She began the careful work of picking apart the stitches that held the plain brown lining to the inner body of the coat. Her hands moving with a steady and deliberate precision that spoke of years of experience. The threads gave way under the sharp point of the tool, parting silently to create a small opening in the fabric seam just large enough for a hand to fit through. Rosa watched this process with a growing sense of confusion. Why would her mother unpick a perfectly good lining on a serviceable coat? Her mother reached into the opening she had created within the coat's inner structure, her fingers searching for something hidden deep within the layers of cloth.

She did not pull out a piece of hidden money or a forgotten letter but instead brought forth a dense weave of many colored threads that glowed in the dim light of the room. The threads were not loose or tangled but were woven together into a complex and tiny tapestry of intricate patterns, a miniature landscape of red, blue, gold and black. Rosa could only stare at the object in her mother's palm, unable to comprehend what she was seeing or what purpose it could possibly serve. Her mother explained that the woven patch was in fact a song, a banned piece of music from another time that had been translated into a new and secret language.

She said the different colors represented the various notes of the musical scale while the complex weave itself held the rhythm and the melody within its structure. This particular pattern was the last movement of the Fourth Symphony, a piece of music that had been officially banned and systematically destroyed by the current authorities. Rosa looked from the woven patch in her mother's hand to the other coats hanging by the front door. A dawning horror and admiration growing within her as she understood the full scope of the project. Her mother confirmed that all the coats contained similar woven patterns within their linings, an entire archive of banned music and forgotten folk songs from the western provinces that she had preserved through this act of silent rebellion.

She had heard these songs and remembered them. Then she translated them into this coded language of thread, creating a portable library of forbidden culture hidden in the one thing everyone owned and needed. The brilliant insanity of the plan took Rosa's breath away even as the terrible danger of it made her heart beat faster within her chest. Her mother began to sew the lining back together with small and nearly invisible stitches, making the evidence of her crime vanish behind a curtain of plain and ordinary brown cloth once more. Two days later there was a polite and quiet knock on the door of the apartment early in the morning, a sound that was somehow more frightening than a shout would have been.

Rosa opened the door to find two men in clean gray uniforms standing in the hallway, their faces blank and their eyes devoid of any recognizable human emotion. One of the men asked for Agata by name, looking past Rosa to where her mother stood waiting as if she had been expecting this visit for a long time. Her mother confirmed her identity and put on her shoes without being asked, deliberately not taking a coat from the hook by the door before walking out into the hallway. The men did not touch her or handcuff her but simply walked on either side of her down the stairs and out of the building, leaving Rosa standing alone in the open doorway.

The silence of the apartment felt different now, charged with a new and terrible meaning that made the air difficult to breathe. Rosa looked at the coats hanging by the door. Her mother's life's work and her dangerous beautiful burden. She felt the weight of that knowledge settle upon her shoulders like a physical thing. Across the city in a different kind of apartment there was another knock on another door, this one answered by a man who had been waiting for this moment with a dull and resigned certainty. Elias opened his door to see the gray uniforms and knew immediately why they had come for him this time, their purpose written in the set of their shoulders and the coldness of their eyes.

They informed him that he was required for a session of clarification regarding certain inconsistencies in his recent work and his personal loyalties. He nodded his understanding of the situation and followed them out into the hallway without looking back at his wife standing in the kitchen doorway with her hand pressed to her mouth. They took him to a white room with a table and two chairs and a bright light overhead that hurt his eyes and made it difficult to think clearly. They asked him questions that had nothing to do with his actual work at the newspaper and everything to do with his private thoughts and his family loyalties and his daughter's activities at college.

He tried at first to be clever with his answers and vague with his details. But their questions were like needles finding the cracks in his composure and prying them open wider and wider. He broke under the pressure more quickly than he would have thought possible. His words spilling out in a desperate flood of confession and invention. He told them about the scrap of paper he had saved from the furnace and about his walk by the river. He told them about the humming in the basement. He gave them names of people he barely knew and names he completely made up just to make the questions stop. When he was finally empty of words and secrets they led him out of the building and put him on the street without another word, leaving him to walk home under a sun that felt too bright and a sky that felt too large.

He felt hollowed out and scraped clean inside, a shell of a man who had confessed to crimes he did not commit to avoid a pain he could not even name. The sound of the hum began to migrate through the city in the days that followed, a ghost of a sound that appeared in unexpected places and at unexpected times. It was heard in an elevator between floors. A single low note hummed by a man facing the doors and picked up by a woman who carried it out with her into the street. It was played on a harmonica on a crowded trolley, just three notes in the familiar pattern before the instrument was pocketed and the player was gone into the crowd.

It was resonated through the trunk of a leafless tree in a public park. A child's hum vibrating through the wood and into the ground beneath. It became a city-wide ritual of silent solidarity. A word passed from one person to another without a single spoken syllable to mark its passage. Rosa heard the hum in the water pipes of her building and in the wind at night outside her window. A ghost of the sound from the basement that had become her mother's lasting legacy to the city. She took a nail and a hammer and went out into the streets to continue the work her mother had started, finding a cobblestone in a quiet square and placing the nail against its surface.

She struck the nail with the hammer just hard enough to leave a small dot in the stone, then moved the nail and struck it again to leave a dash beside the dot. She stamped out the entire word in this Morse code of sound and stone, a pattern of dots and dashes that spelled *remember* for anyone who knew how to read it. The marks were small and faint and looked like natural flaws in the stone to the casual observer, but they were there waiting for someone to find them. She found a metal railing and stamped the word into the chipped paint, and she found a wooden bench and carved it into the grain of the wood.

She was creating a new kind of network across the city. A map of sound waiting to be played by someone with the right kind of ears to hear it. The city itself was slowly becoming a giant instrument for resistance. A library of defiance written in code upon its skin for future generations to discover and decipher. She worked quickly and without looking around at the people passing by on the street, knowing the risk she was taking with every strike of her hammer against the nail. The work itself was a balm for the silence her mother had left behind. A promise that the songs were not gone but merely waiting for the right moment to be played again.

The guard who had been watching her from across the square would make a note of her actions in his daily report. A report that would be filed under the number 8647 for future reference.

The arrest of Agata was not an isolated event. It was part of a new, targeted campaign. The raid on the button factory had been a blunt instrument; this was a surgical strike. The regime, unnerved by the persistence of the humming and the symbols, had tasked its most insidious organ with a response: the *Bureau of Counter Intelligence.* The BCI's approach was not to break down doors, but to follow threads. They analyzed patterns, informant reports, and intercepted whispers. Agata's name had likely emerged from the confession of a broken soul like Elias, or from a neighbor who had grown suspicious of the woman who never threw away an old coat.

Rosa, in her grief and fury, became a nexus for *The Undercurrent.* The quiet network, which had been a loose collection of disaffected individuals, now began to coalesce around her. It was Mira who found her, two days after Agata was taken. She had heard the story through the whisper-web—a woman taken for the music in her seams. Mira arrived at Rosa's door with a loaf of black bread, a gesture of solidarity. She didn't offer empty comfort. Instead, she showed Rosa the small jar with the blood-smeared label in her bag. "They take our people," Mira said, her voice low and steady. "We remember them. That is the work."

This was how The Undercurrent grew: not through grand speeches, but through shared pain and silent recognition. A man who repaired shoes began etching the wave symbol into the inner sole of the left shoe of every pair he fixed. A washerwoman at the public baths hummed the sequence as she worked, the steam carrying the sound. The network's strength was its diffuseness. It had no central leader, but it had hearts like Rosa's apartment, where the archive of woven songs was now hidden under the floorboards.

Elias, meanwhile, lived in a different kind of silence. His "clarification" had left him psychologically flayed. He walked through the city like a ghost, seeing the new symbols—the dots and dashes on the cobblestones, the wave on the walls—with a crushing sense of guilt. He had likely given them Agata's name. He had certainly given them others. Every hum he heard was an accusation. He was given a new assignment at the *Beacon*: to write a series of articles decrying the "rising tide of dissonant thought" and praising the *Bureau of Belligerent Blunder Heads* for their "vigilant protection of our harmonic unity." The irony was exquisite and torturous. He was to use his pen to attack the very thing he had helped create and now desperately wished to join.

The regime's response was multifaceted. The BCI worked in the shadows, while the Blunder Heads provided the public face of the crackdown. They announced a new "Public Harmony Act," which made "the unauthorized transmission of coded auditory signals" a crime punishable by re-education. They didn't understand the resistance, so they tried to legislate against sound itself.

But they could not police every hum, every glance, every symbol scratched in a hidden place. The *Tower of Song* continued its eternal broadcast, and now the people's hum had become a quiet, earthly echo of its haunting melodies. The resistance was no longer just about remembering the past; it was about asserting a present reality that the regime could not control. It was in the hum of a factory worker, the stitch of a seamstress, the mark of a cobbler. It was the sound of a people, slowly and silently, tuning themselves to a different frequency. And Rosa, with her hammer and nail, was their cartographer, mapping the way to a future built not on the Leader's progress, but on the people's memory.

Chapter 3

The Hall of Historical Correction existed as a vast and chillingly silent space where the very air seemed unwilling to move. A stagnant atmosphere that felt heavy with official condemnation and deliberate forgetting. Flat and artificial light fell in sterile beams from high narrow windows onto rows of glass display cases that lined the cold marble floors, illuminating the objects trapped within for public scrutiny. Each case contained a single artifact from the time before the current administration. Ordinary things like a painted plate, a child's wooden toy or a book with a colorful cover. Each item labeled with a small printed card that explained its inherent moral failure. The cards spoke of decadence and subversion and weakness, transforming the museum from a place of history into a place of perpetual warning against the dangers of the past.

Mira pushed a large cleaning cart slowly through the echoing halls. The wheels making a soft and rhythmic sound against the polished floor that seemed too loud in the overwhelming quiet. The cart carried a bucket of soapy water and a stack of clean cloths for wiping away fingerprints and dust from the glass surfaces of the display cases. Her official job was to maintain the cleanliness and brightness of these warnings for the public, but she tried not to look too closely at the objects inside the cases for very long. She understood these items were meant as reminders of a world they said was sick and broken. A world that required the harsh medicine of the present to cure its many illnesses.

A man wearing the standard gray tunic of a museum curator approached her cart with a cardboard box held in his hands, his expression one of profound bureaucratic boredom. He told her these were new acquisitions from the most recent round of clarifications. He handed her the box with instructions to catalog each item and assign it to a suitable display case. She took the surprisingly light box and carried it to a small back room that contained only a single wooden table and a bare light bulb hanging from a wire overhead. She opened the cardboard flaps. She looked inside at the collection of small personal effects that had once belonged to people who were now gone.

The box contained the ordinary things people carried in their pockets and purses every day. A pocket watch, a pair of spectacles, a simple wedding band and a small notebook with blank pages. These objects were the physical remains of the disappeared, the clarified, the people who had been erased from the present for their failures to conform. She removed each item one by one and wrote a brief description on an official form. She assigned it a number and considered which case might best display the error of the person who had owned it. Near the bottom of the box her fingers touched something cold and metallic, and she pulled out a press badge with a name she recognized engraved upon its surface.

She held the badge in her hand and felt the cool weight of the metal against her skin. Thinking of the journalist who had written for the Beacon and who had burned things in a basement furnace. She wondered what specific confession he had offered during his own clarification, what words he had spoken to make them let him go. She placed the badge on the table and finished cataloging the rest of the items from the box, saving the badge for last as if delaying its fate might change something. When the box was empty she picked up the badge again and knew she should assign it a number and find a case for it like all the other objects.

She did not do what she was supposed to do with the badge. Instead slipping it into the pocket of her cleaning uniform where it rested as a small and secret weight against her leg. She finished her work for the day and pushed her cart back out into the main hall of the museum. A few silent people moved through the rooms looking at the cases with blank expressions. She noticed a young girl of about ten years standing perfectly still in front of a case that contained a man's leather wallet. Tears rolling down her face without a sound as she stared at the object behind the glass.

Mira stopped her cart and looked at the girl for a long moment, recognizing the particular look of a child who has lost someone important and can't understand why. The girl noticed Mira looking at her but did not turn away or try to hide her tears. Her eyes full of a deep and quiet hurt that needed no explanation. Mira walked over to the girl without speaking and reached into her pocket for the press badge. She held it out in her open palm for the girl to see. The girl looked at the badge and then at Mira's face. Her expression one of confusion about this unexpected offering.

Mira told the girl in a soft voice that the badge had belonged to someone and now it belonged to her. A simple statement of transfer that felt more meaningful than it should. The girl's fingers closed around the metal badge and held it tightly in her small fist, nodding once before turning to walk away without a word of thanks. Several days passed in the usual routine of cleaning glass cases and mopping floors, but Mira found herself thinking about the girl and the badge more often than she expected. One morning on her way to work her feet carried her down the street where she thought the girl might live. A detour she had not consciously planned but felt compelled to make.

She saw the concrete steps of a small apartment building and noticed a clay pot sitting on the top step with a geranium plant growing inside it. The plant had vibrant green leaves and a single bright red flower blooming at its center, a spot of color against the gray concrete. Something metal was partially buried in the dark soil near the base of the plant, catching the morning light in a familiar way. Mira stopped walking and looked more closely at the pot, recognizing the press badge she had given the girl now planted in the dirt like a seed.

The badge was half-covered by the rich soil with the healthy plant growing boldly around it, the leaves and flowers seeming to thrive in this unlikely place. Mira stood on the sidewalk and stared at this unexpected transformation of a symbol of complicity into part of something living and growing. She noticed a curtain moving in a window of the building and saw the girl's face looking out at her for a moment before the curtain fell back into place. Mira continued on her way to the museum and performed her cleaning duties as usual, but the image of the badge in the soil stayed with her throughout the day.

Over the following week she found herself taking the same route to work each morning, noticing that other people sometimes paused near the steps to look at the plant. A woman would stop for a moment to adjust her scarf while her eyes studied the geranium, or a man would pause to tie his shoe while glancing at the pot. They never stayed long and they never spoke to one another, but they came and looked as if drawn by some silent understanding of what the plant represented. The geranium continued to grow larger and stronger with each passing day, its leaves spreading wider and more flowers blooming in defiant red bursts. It soon covered the badge completely with its growth, but everyone who looked at it knew exactly what was buried there beneath the living green. The guard who patrolled that street would later file a routine report about the plant, a report that would be assigned the number 8647 and placed in a file that nobody would ever read.

Mira's work at the *Hall of Historical Correction* was a daily exercise in cognitive dissonance. She would spend her mornings polishing the glass that protected state-sanctioned lies. Her mind echoing with the words from the small, typewritten cards she had to clean around: "This children's book promoted unrealistic dreams and weakened the collective resolve." "This pair of blue jeans represents the decadent importation of foreign cultural weakness." The sheer, breathtaking pettiness of it was its most insidious quality. It wasn't just about rewriting grand history; it was about pathologizing everyday life, making the past a place of shame.

Her cart's route often took her past the Hall's research annex, a place the junior curators called *The Misinformation Center*. This was where the real, unedited books were kept before they were pulped or locked away in permanent archives. Sometimes, a door would be left ajar, and she would catch a glimpse of towering shelves crammed with beautiful, colorful spines—a shocking contrast to the sparse, curated hatefulness of the public displays. The smell of old paper and glue that wafted out was the smell of a world that had been murdered. She understood now that this entire building, from the public halls to the locked library, was a tomb and she was its custodian.

The encounter with the girl and the subsequent discovery of the geranium pot ignited a new, dangerous impulse in her. She began her own small, silent corrections. While dusting a case that displayed a well-worn cookbook as an example of "enslaving women to domesticity," she used a tiny sliver of soapstone to add a nearly invisible mark to the corner of the glass—a small 'X'. It meant nothing to anyone else, but to her, it was a flag, a way of marking the lie. She did it not knowing if anyone would ever notice, but the act itself was a reclamation of her own mind.

She soon discovered she was not alone. A week after marking the cookbook case, she found a different mark waiting for her on the glass of a display containing a banned jazz record—a tiny, etched wave, the symbol of *The Undercurrent*. Her heart hammered against her ribs. The resistance was here, inside the very heart of the regime's fortress of lies. Another cleaner? A curator? It didn't matter. The symbol was a message: *I see your mark. I am here too.*

This silent communication within the Hall of Historical Correction became a new layer of the resistance. The public displays, intended to be monolithic and authoritative, were now being subtly tagged, critiqued, and contradicted from within by the very people paid to maintain them. The Hall, designed to be the final word on the past, was instead becoming a palimpsest. Its official narrative overwritten with tiny, defiant scratches of truth.

The geranium pot, meanwhile, had become an unlikely landmark. People began to leave small offerings. A smooth, gray river stone appeared beside it one day. A few days later, a single, fresh dandelion was tucked into its soil. These were not acts of grand vandalism, but of tender cultivation. They were watering the truth, ensuring it grew. The pot was a living rebuttal to the dead, glassed-in world of the Hall. It was proof that memory, when planted, could take root and flourish, even in the most barren of concrete landscapes. The regime could lock away books and display stolen wallets, but it could not stop a flower from blooming over a secret. Mira realized this was the core of The Undercurrent's power: it didn't attack the regime's lies head-on; it simply planted truths and let them grow, quietly and indestructibly, all on their own.

Chapter 4

The news of the Leader's passing did not arrive through any official channel or public announcement, but instead manifested as a profound and city-wide silence that fell over everything like a heavy blanket. The trolleys continued their routes and people still walked to their destinations, but the very air itself felt different without the constant pressure of his presence. It was a physical change that every person could feel in their bones, a sudden and unsettling absence of the force that had defined their lives for so many years. People looked at each other on the streets and in the shops with questioning eyes that asked the same thing without speaking a single word. They all wondered what would happen now that the engine of their world had gone cold.

In a quiet and secure room somewhere in the government district, a group of men in dark suits sat around a polished table, their expressions not of grief but of urgent calculation. The Leader was gone and with him the central symbol of their power structure. Leaving them with a dangerous vacuum that needed immediate filling. They understood that this silence in the streets could not be allowed to last for long before people began to realize their cage door might actually be open. One of the men spoke in a low and urgent voice about the necessity of replacement, about the critical importance of maintaining the structure they had built together.

Another man nodded his agreement and stated that their new figurehead could not be a conventional politician but must be a voice and a presence that people would follow without question. They needed someone who spoke the same language of strength and simple truths that their followers had come to expect and demand from their leadership. A third man quietly corrected that it was really a language of simple lies they needed, but no one at the table acknowledged his uncomfortable observation. They began compiling a list of potential candidates who could stand where he had stood and look out from that high window with the same cold eye, someone who understood that facts were less important than faith in their continued authority.

While these men planned for the future of their power structure, the entire city seemed to hold its collective breath in anticipation of what might come next. Elias walked slowly toward the river with heavy footsteps and an even heavier heart. His body still carrying the trauma of his recent clarification session. He felt completely hollowed out by the experience. Reduced to a shell of a man who had confessed to crimes both real and imagined in his desperation. The guilt sat like a stone in his stomach and the shame left a permanent taste in his mouth that nothing could remove, driving him toward the water with a single purpose.

He stood on the muddy bank and looked at the brown water moving slowly past, a force of nature that did not care about his pain or his existence. He stepped into the cold water and felt it soak through his shoes and pants as he moved deeper into the current that pulled at his legs. He continued walking until the water closed over his head and the world became dark and silent around him, opening his mouth to let the river fill his lungs and wash him clean of everything. But the river seemed to reject his offering, changing its current to push him across the water rather than down into the mud.

He found himself washed onto a shallow sandbar he had never noticed before. Coughing up water as he lay on his back looking at the gray sky above. He sat up in the shallow water and looked around at the water lilies growing in a patch around him. Their white flowers open on broad green leaves. Each lily held a small square piece of paper that he recognized as his own ration coupons that must have fallen from his pocket during his immersion. The river water had washed the printing completely clean from the coupons, leaving them blank and pure white as they floated in the flowers like bizarre offerings.

He picked one of the coupons from a lily and held the wet blank paper in his hand, trying to make sense of what had happened to him. He had tried to end his life and the world had refused his attempt. Spitting him back onto the bank with this strange and life-affirming joke that defied all explanation. He stood up dripping and cold but undeniably alive. Feeling the emptiness inside him that was now just emptiness without the guilt or shame that had filled it before. The space inside him waited now for something new to fill it. Something that had not existed before his rejection by the river.

Rosa heard the news from a neighbor who whispered the words in the hallway outside her apartment. A simple statement that he was gone now. She stood in her small living space and looked at her mother's empty chair and at the coats hanging by the door that contained the archive of threads. The weight of her grief pressed physically on her chest and demanded some kind of answer or expression that she could not contain within herself any longer. She left her apartment and walked to the old button factory with its shattered basement and broken door, going inside to search for something she could use.

She found a length of copper tubing and a discarded metal plate amid the ruins of the place where they had made music together, taking these scraps home with a determined purpose. She used a hammer and a nail to beat the copper into shape, bending and forming the metal into a crude horn that resembled a saxophone made of anger and grief. Her hands became cut and her arms ached from the effort but she did not stop working until the instrument was complete in its brutal and ugly form. She put the makeshift mouthpiece to her lips without knowing how to play properly and blew a single raw and screaming note into the silence of her apartment.

The sound that emerged was not music but pure anguish given audible form. A requiem for her lost mother and a funeral dirge for the era that had taken her away. She played the note until her lungs were completely empty and then stopped to let the sound hang in the air before fading away. The scream now released from her body and set loose in the world where it could exist independently of her. Mira stood in her own apartment looking at the museum uniform hanging on its hook by the door, a gray symbol of her compliance and daily betrayal of truth. She took the uniform down and folded it carefully before lighting a burner on her small stove and holding the cloth over the flame.

The fabric caught fire quickly and burned with orange and blue flames that turned it to ash in the metal basin she held beneath it. The smoke filling the room with the smell of burning cotton and personal release. She carried the basin to her window and opened it to let the smoke drift out into the city air where it mingled with the strange silence that had fallen over everything. She was no longer a cleaner of lies but someone actively unbecoming what they had made her, sending a signal of her transformation out into the waiting city. She stood at the window until the last of the smoke had dissipated into the air. Watching the clear sky that held both fear and hope for whatever would come next. The paperwork for her employment termination would eventually be processed under file number 8647, a number that would no longer have any meaning or power over her life.

The silence that followed the Leader's death was not truly silent. It was a silence of held breath, of paused mechanisms, of waiting. It was most profound near the *Cathedral of Silence*. For days, its great doors remained shut, its custodians uncertain of the proper protocol for mourning a god who had claimed not to die. The absolute auditory void within its walls seemed to seep out into the surrounding streets, making them quieter, more spectral. People gave it a wide berth, as if the building itself were a corpse.

In stark contrast, the *Tower of Song* seemed to gain a new power. Its eternal melodies, usually a source of melancholy beauty, now felt prophetic, elegiac, and strangely triumphant. It played a slow, stately processional that some of the elders recognized as a funeral march from a time before the Leader. The Tower, as always, reflected the soul of the city back at itself. It was the one voice that could not be commanded to mourn or to celebrate, and so it did both, and neither, simply bearing witness as it always had.

This silence was a vacuum, and *The Undercurrent* moved to fill it. The news had traveled through its channels faster than through the official ones. In the back room of the *Jazz Club*, there was no celebration, only a swift, serious meeting. The owner, a man named Warryn, laid out the reality. "The head is gone, but the body is twitching. The Bureau of Belligerent Blunder Heads will be fighting for control. The Bureau of Counter Intelligence will be hunting for scapegoats. This is the most dangerous time. When a system dies, it thrashes."

Mira, her apartment still smelling of smoke, knew he was right. She had seen the men in suits arriving at the *Hall of Historical Corrections* in unmarked cars, moving with a new urgency. They were likely inside right now. Scrubbing the Leader's minor errors from the record. Preparing to canonize him as a flawless martyr. The work of building the lie was continuing even before the body was cold.

Rosa's scream from her scrap-metal saxophone had been a necessary, personal catharsis. But the next day, she returned to the button factory basement. This time, she did not go alone. She brought a small, trusted group from The Undercurrent. They spent the day not making music, but clearing the wreckage. They swept up the broken glass, straightened the overturned crates, and patched the broken door as best they could. It was not an act of defiance, but of preparation. The silence was an intermission, not an ending. They would need a place to gather again, to decide what sound to make next.

Elias, meanwhile, walked back into the city from the river, a dripping, shambling mess. People glanced at him but looked away quickly; strangeness was to be avoided. He passed the *Library of Errors*, its doors still chained. He had a mad thought: was every book in there still wrong, now that the author of those errors was gone? Or had their wrongness been somehow confirmed? The world had not magically righted itself. The infrastructure of oppression—the Bureaus, the Halls, the Libraries—remained. He had been rejected by the water, but the city he returned to was the same. And yet, it wasn't. The center was gone. Everything felt loose, unmoored, and terrifyingly possible.

That night, for the first time, the hum did not sound. The Undercurrent was silent, listening. They were waiting to see what the morning would bring. Would it be a new face on the posters, a new voice from the loudspeakers? Or would the silence hold? The city was balanced on a knife-edge between a past that was not yet dead and a future that was not yet born. And in that precarious space, every single person, from the highest functionary to the lowliest cleaner, was holding their breath, waiting to see which way they would fall.

Chapter 5

The scrap-metal saxophone lay abandoned in the darkest corner of the derelict basement where Rosa had left it, a silent monument to her single moment of audible grief. She had not touched the instrument since the day she played its one raw note into the waiting silence of the broken button factory. The day it expelled the scream that had been building inside her for months. The crude copper tubing began to oxidize in the damp air of the basement. A green patina slowly spreading across its surface like a new kind of skin. The metal plate she had hammered into shape developed streaks of brown rust that ran down its sides like tears. The entire instrument gradually returning to the earth from which its materials had come. The crickets found it weeks later, emerging from the cracks in the foundation and the dark corners where moisture collected.

They were small brown insects that moved with quick and jerky steps across the concrete floor, exploring this new metal landscape that had appeared in their territory. One cricket discovered the saxophone's bell and crawled inside the sheltered space that remained dry despite the basement's dampness, deciding to make its home within the instrument's corpse. Others soon followed this pioneer until a small colony had established itself within the copper tubing, transforming the object into an unlikely habitat. At dusk they began their nightly chirping. The sound emerging from within the metal body that amplified and resonated their calls until the basement filled with a new kind of music. The fossilized scream of grief had been reborn as an organic insect song, a chorus of life emerging from what had been left for dead.

Mira heard whispers about the basement from people in her neighborhood, about the strange music that could be heard there after dark. She went to investigate one evening carrying a small tin that contained the ashes of her burned museum uniform. The physical remains of her compliance with the regime's lies. She stood in the broken doorway and listened to the crickets making their lively static sound in the quiet dark. A sound that felt both ancient and completely new. She saw the rusted saxophone now alive with movement and sound. This transformation of anger into something natural and persistent. She opened her tin and stepped forward to sprinkle the ashes over the instrument. The gray powder dusting the rusted metal and settling into its grooves like a blessing.

She was feeding this new form of resistance with the remains of her old compliance. Acknowledging that the past could become fertilizer for whatever might grow next. She turned and left the basement without looking back. The crickets continuing their song without pause or recognition of her presence. Mrs. Nova walked through Cathedral Square on her way to collect her daily rations, keeping her eyes on the pavement as had become her habit over the years. She had not looked directly at the great stained-glass eye in a very long time. She had grown accustomed to feeling its gaze upon her without meeting it with her own. Today felt different somehow, with the Leader gone and the air itself feeling lighter. The eye seemed less like a living thing and more like simple colored glass held together with lead.

She stopped in the middle of the empty square. She made herself look up at the enormous window that dominated the entire façade of the Cathedral. The eye that had been meant to inspire awe and fear in equal measure. She felt neither of these things now. Only a small and sharp anger that made her remember the taste of sugar and the sound of a neighbor's radio that had gone silent. She walked to the base of the Cathedral. Scaffolding from the original construction still leaned against the wall in a few places. She looked around to confirm the square was empty before acting. She climbed onto a low ledge and reached up until her fingers touched the bottom edge of the stained glass, feeling the thick pieces and the solid lead between them.

She found a small piece near the corner that had worked loose from its setting. A shard of blue iris glass that felt sharp and cool against her skin. She worked at it with her fingernails until it came free and fell into her waiting palm, a piece of the eye now separated from the whole. She closed her hand around it and stepped down from the ledge, walking away without looking back at the damage she had caused. She had taken a piece of the gaze that had judged her for so long, diminishing its power in this small and personal act of defiance. The glass shard in her pocket felt like a weight and a trophy all at once, a tangible piece of her reclamation.

High above on the Cathedral's spire, pigeons continued their daily routines of nesting and feeding in the crooks and ledges of the stonework. They were not concerned with the meaning or symbolism of the structure beneath them, living their simple lives according to their own needs and instincts. Their droppings fell regularly on the stained-glass eye below. Acidic white streaks that painted the blue iris, green pupil and red veins with abstract patterns. The acid slowly ate at the glass surface over days and then weeks, etching permanent marks into the expensive imported materials. The weather helped this process along with rain washing dirt into the etched lines and the sun baking it all into place, wind adding dust to darken the emerging patterns.

One morning the sun rose particularly bright and clear. Its light hitting the eye at such an angle that the stains became legible as words for the first time. Two words had been etched into the glass by chance and nature and time, visible now to anyone who bothered to look up at the façade. People in the square noticed the words throughout the day. Stopping in their tracks to point and stare without speaking to each other about what they were seeing. The words hung over the city as both statement and question. A promise, a message from nature itself on the face of human power. The regime's leader was dead and his symbols were decaying around them. Leaving the city in that fragile space between captivity and freedom.

The future remained unknown, dangerous and hopeful all at once. The silence of transition holding everyone in a state of breathless anticipation. Something would inevitably fill this silence sooner or later, but for now the city existed in that almost state. Poised on the edge of whatever might come next. The paperwork for repairing the Cathedral damage would be filed under number 8647, a number that seemed increasingly meaningless as the structures it represented continued to crumble.

The decay was not just physical; it was institutional. Within the halls of power, a frantic, silent scramble was underway. The *Bureau of Belligerent Blunder Heads*, suddenly without its central figurehead, was like a headless chicken, running in circles and squawking contradictory orders. They argued over who should sit at the Leader's old desk in *The Light House*, their belligerence now turned inward, their blunders multiplying in the vacuum. They issued a flurry of new directives about mandatory mourning periods and the proper display of the Leader's portrait, but their words had lost their weight. The trolleys still ran, but fewer people bothered to look at the new posters they slapped up.

The *Bureau of Counter Intelligence* reacted differently. They became quieter, more sinister, more dangerous. They understood that their power had never truly come from the Leader himself, but from the *system* of control. And that system was still intact. They redoubled their efforts, not to find a new leader, but to contain the spread of what they called "the contagion of freedom." Their agents were everywhere, listening for the hum, watching for the symbols. The silence of the population was not trust; it was a terrified pause. The BCI was the deep state, and it was ensuring it would outlive its creator.

Meanwhile, *The Undercurrent* did not rush. They watched the pigeons deface the Cathedral. They heard the crickets in the basement. They saw the geranium thriving on its steps. They understood something the Bureaus did not: that time was on their side. The regime's power had been a performance, and the main actor had left the stage. The stagehands were now fighting over the spotlight, but the audience was already getting up to leave.

Rosa, guided by the more experienced members of the network, began a new project. Using the patterns her mother had taught her, she didn't just stitch the word *remember* anymore. She began stitching maps. Tiny, coded diagrams of the city's infrastructure—water pipes, electrical conduits, old steam tunnels— were woven into the linings of coats that were then "donated" to distribution centers for the poor. These were maps of the city's veins and arteries, knowledge that could be vital. The *Institution of Heretical Science*, though still officially demonized, became an unwitting ally. Its shunned researchers, who understood how things actually worked, were often the source of this practical, truthful information that now flowed through The Undercurrent's covert channels.

The city was in a state of unraveling. An unbecoming. The grandiose, top-down control of the Leader was being replaced by a million small, quiet, bottom-up acts of reclamation. A child's red balloon, caught on the spire of the *Tower of Song*, looked from a distance like a second, smaller sun—a brief, beautiful mistake that no one in authority bothered to correct. In the *Library of Errors*, a cleaner (not Mira, but perhaps someone she had inspired) began re-shelving books according to the Dewey Decimal System instead of the state-approved "Ideological Purity Index." It was a small act, but it was an act of restoration.

The words etched on the Cathedral's eye—*ALMOST FREE*—were not a promise. They were an observation. The 'almost' was the most important part. It acknowledged the fear, the lingering power of the Bureaus, the uncertainty of what came next. But it also acknowledged the 'free' as an inevitable fact, already in progress, already being built in the rusting saxophones, the growing plants, the mapped coat linings, and the silent, watchful patience of those who had learned to outlast the noise.

Part III

Chapter 1

The river moved with a slow and purposeful current that carried the forgotten things of the city along its brown water. A continuous flow of mud and branches and lost objects heading toward some unknown destination. A solitary man walked along the muddy bank with his eyes fixed on the ground. His dusty clothes and old pack suggesting he was not from this place but just passing through on his journey. He noticed a peculiar shape partially buried in the thick mud near the water's edge. Something too regular and structured to be just another stone or piece of driftwood. He knelt down in the damp earth and dug with his bare fingers until he could pull the object free from its clinging embrace, washing it in the river to clear away the layers of accumulated dirt and sediment.

The object revealed itself as a hardened lump of metal and organic material fused together by time and pressure. A press badge and a key bound together by the fine dry roots of what must have been a plant. The roots had grown around and through the metal objects during some period of burial, creating a single fossilized artifact that spoke of connection and memory. The man carried this strange find to a clear spot on the bank where he gathered dry grass and twigs into a small pile, placing the fused object carefully on top of this makeshift altar. He struck a match and lit the dry tinder, watching as the flames caught and began to consume the grass and twigs with crackling intensity.

The roots and metal heated in the growing fire, the organic material blackening and smoking rather than burning cleanly away. The smoke rose in a thick white column that seemed to hang together in the air instead of immediately dispersing on the wind. Forming shapes and letters that resolved into words. A name and a phrase became visible in the smoke for just a moment before the wind finally took them. A declaration that could not be unmade once it had been made. The man watched this phenomenon without smiling or showing any particular emotion. Simply nodding once before turning to continue his journey along the riverbank.

Mira stood further down the bank where she had come to watch the water as had become her habit these days. She witnessed the entire ritual from a distance without interrupting. She recognized the name that had formed in the smoke. The journalist who had broken under pressure and whom the river had rejected when he tried to end his life. The word that had followed his name felt strange yet appropriate, suggesting that his story was not over and his record was not erased despite what had been done to him. His complicity and his suffering remained part of the history that could not be unmade. A truth that was now re-entering the world whether anyone was ready for it or not.

She looked at the small circle of ash left where the fire had burned, a physical fact that could not be denied or ignored no matter how inconvenient it might prove to be. She turned away from the river and walked back toward the city with this new knowledge settling inside her. Another piece of the puzzle that was their collective experience. Rosa walked through the abandoned botanical gardens where nature had reclaimed the paths and structures with relentless green determination. Plants growing wild over broken benches and through cracked concrete. She had come looking for silence and space away from the city's breathless waiting for what might happen next. A place to think without the pressure of all those watching eyes.

She noticed a tree she did not recognize with long dry seedpods hanging from its branches like brown teardrops waiting to fall, reaching up to take one and examine it more closely. The pod felt rough in her hand. It's surface was not smooth but covered in small bumps arranged in deliberate patterns rather than random formations. She realized these bumps formed a coded language of dots that spelled out a word she knew well. The same word that had been tapped on water glasses and stamped on stones throughout the city. The tree remembered and carried this memory in its seeds. A scripture waiting to be carried on the wind to whoever might find it and understand its message.

A girl stepped out from behind another tree with a basket full of foraged roots and leaves. Her patched clothes suggesting she knew how to live with what nature provided. She told Rosa that her grandfather had created these seedpods before they took him away, using his skills as a printer to carve words and attach them to trees that would grow around them. The trees made these words part of their seeds so they could be carried on the wind for others to find and remember. What her grandfather had called brown scriptures that would outlive them all. The girl reached into her basket and brought out another longer pod with more complex bumps that contained a message she had not yet fully deciphered, holding it out to Rosa as an offering.

Rosa took the heavy pod and closed her fingers around its meaningful surface. She felt the truth within that could be planted and grown rather than simply spoken or written. The girl nodded once before turning to disappear back into the green shadows of the garden. Leaving Rosa alone with this new responsibility and possibility. The report of this unusual interaction would eventually be filed under number 8647 by a watchful guard. But the number would have no power over what had been set in motion here among the trees and the seeds that knew how to remember what humans so often forgot.

The city was breathing differently. The constant, low-grade fear that had been the atmosphere of life under the Leader was dissipating, replaced by a watchful, fragile curiosity. *The Undercurrent* was no longer just a whisper; it was becoming a nervous system for the city, connecting people and information with a speed that the crumbling bureaucracies could no longer match.

The man by the river was part of this. He was a "walker," one of a growing number of people who moved between the city's fragments, carrying news and objects too sensitive for any other method. He had known Elias, had heard the story of the scrap of paper and the river. His ritual with the fused object was not just personal; it was a form of communication, a way of sending a message on the wind, trusting that the right person would see it. He was a living testament to the fact that the *Bureau of Counter Intelligence* had failed. They could monitor wires and intercept letters, but they could not stop a man from kneeling by a river and letting smoke carry a truth.

Mira, watching from a distance, understood this. Her days of collecting ash were over. Now, she was learning to read the new language of the city. The message in the smoke was one sign. The geranium plant, now enormous and spilling gloriously over its pot, was another. People left small tokens at its base—a button, a scrap of ribbon, a single cog from a broken machine—a quiet altar to persistence. The *Hall of Historical Correction* was still open, but fewer people visited. Why look at curated lies in glass cases when truth was growing, wild and abundant, right outside your door?

Rosa's discovery in the botanical gardens felt like a culmination. The old man, the printer, had been a heretic of the highest order. While the regime was building the *Library of Errors*, he had been creating a living library, using nature itself as his printing press and distribution system. His "brown scriptures" were the ultimate rebuttal to the state's control of information. You could burn a book, but how do you burn a seed? How do you arrest the wind?

Rosa carried the heavy seedpod back to the button factory basement, which had become The Undercurrent's de facto workshop. Under the light of a single, shadeless bulb, she and others—including Mira now—pored over the pod. Using a magnifying glass and a chart of Morse code, they slowly decoded the longer message. It was not a single word, but a sequence, a set of instructions. Coordinates. Dates. It was a map to other caches, other hidden things the old printer had seeded throughout the city and beyond.

The girl in the garden had been one of many "foragers" who knew of these treasures. She was part of a network that existed entirely outside the city's official structures. A network of people who looked to the natural world for guidance and truth. They knew which mushrooms were safe to eat when rations were short, which roots could be used for medicine when the clinics turned you away, and which seeds carried messages from the past.

The regime had tried to build an empire of steel and ideas, but it was proving to be a cage of rust and lies. The future, Rosa realized, holding the seedpod, was not going to be won in a battle against the *Bureau of Belligerent Blunder Heads*. It was going to be grown, slowly and patiently, from seeds planted long ago, nurtured in secret, and now pushing their green shoots through every crack in the concrete. The city wasn't being liberated; it was being pollinated.

Chapter 2

The pigeons abandoned their nests on the Cathedral spire in a single coordinated movement one morning. Rising into the air as a great gray cloud that did not circle or hesitate but flew straight east toward the city's edge. They left behind the stained-glass eye with its etched message and flew toward the abandoned granite quarry that gaped like a wound in the earth beyond the last streets. The quarry presented a vast bowl of exposed rock with steep sheer cliffs of gray stone rising from a flat plain of dust and rubble at the bottom. A place that had not been built but rather unbuilt through decades of extraction. It stood as a monument to what had been taken away rather than what had been constructed. A negative space that spoke of absence rather than presence.

The pigeons settled on the high ledges of the quarry walls in the thousands. Filling the enormous space with their soft cooing that immediately began to transform in the unique acoustics. The sound echoed off the stone walls and amplified itself. Deepening into a rolling drone that merged all individual coos into a single resonant hum. This natural chorus created a sound of profound peace that filled the giant stone bowl. An amen not spoken by human voices but generated by the collective life of creatures that had chosen this place over the human-made one. Rosa felt the vibration of this sound through the soles of her feet while in her apartment. A deep hum that seemed to pull at her very bones with its intensity.

She put down the seedpod she had been studying and left her building without conscious decision. She followed the feeling that guided her footsteps toward the source of this phenomenon. Mira experienced the same pull while sorting through her bag of collected residues. Feeling the hum in the air that made her go to her window and then out her door toward the city's edge. They arrived at the quarry rim separately and looked down into the great bowl where the sound washed over them with physical force. They recognized the hum from the basement but it was transformed into something ancient and eternal by its scale and source. They saw the pigeons covering the cliffs like a living extension of the rock itself, understanding that this place represented the absolute opposite of the Cathedral in every meaningful way.

Where the Cathedral had been built to impress and dominate through human will, the quarry stood as an honest absence that celebrated erosion and the slow undeniable force of decay. Mira climbed down the dusty path to the quarry floor and took a small vial from her bag to collect some of the fine gray powder that coated everything. Adding this quarry dust to her collection as another layer of verdict residue from the world's testimony. Mrs. Nova arrived later and stood on the rim looking down at the two women and the pigeons and their rolling amen. Her eyes eventually finding the shape of the rusted scrap-metal saxophone lying on a flat rock near the bottom. She recognized the relic of raw human grief that had once produced a single scream of pain but now lay silent and subsumed by this larger natural hum. The individual pain not gone but becoming part of something much bigger and older than itself.

The sound continued to roll through the quarry and out into the surrounding area. A vibration that could be felt in the ground and in the bones of anyone who stopped to notice it. A constant reminder that some things could not be controlled or contained no matter how hard anyone tried. The saxophone remained where it lay as the light began to fade from the sky. Its metal cooling as the pigeons settled deeper into their ledges for the night, their collective voice continuing its endless amen into the growing darkness.

The journey to the quarry became a silent pilgrimage. People didn't speak of it; they simply felt the pull and followed it. They came alone, in pairs, in small family groups, all drawn by the sound they could feel in their teeth. They were office workers from the *Bureau of Belligerent Blunder Heads* who'd spent the day writing memos about productivity quotas. They were mechanics from the trolley depot. They were mothers with silent, wide-eyed children. They were even a few gray-faced functionaries from the *Hall of Historical Corrections*, still smelling of dust and disinfectant, seeking something their life's work had deliberately destroyed.

They stood on the rim, as Mrs. Nova did, or they climbed down into the bowl, as Mira had. And they listened. This was not a rally. There were no speeches. The *Tower of Song*, visible in the distance, seemed to be playing in harmony with the quarry's deep hum. A call and response across the city between the man-made and the natural. The sound washed over them, and for the first time in years, perhaps in their entire lives, they experienced a sound that asked nothing of them. It wasn't trying to sell them anything, command them, or frighten them. It simply *was*. It was the sound of existence, vast and unconcerned with their petty human dramas.

For The Undercurrent, this was a moment of profound validation. Their quiet hum, born in a basement, had found its echo in the world itself. The quarry was the perfect cathedral for their movement. It was a place of extraction, of taking, now being filled with a sound of pure, giving presence. It was the opposite of the *Cathedral of Silence*, which sought to absorb all sound and meaning. This place amplified it.

Rosa did not hum. She sat on the dusty ground, the precious seedpod in her lap, and simply cried. It was not the harsh, angry sobbing from after her mother's arrest, but a quiet, releasing flow of tears. The sound of the pigeons was the most beautiful thing she had ever heard because it was utterly useless. It served no purpose for the state. It couldn't be taxed, put to work, or weaponized. It was a gift.

Mira understood this too. She held her vial of quarry dust. This wasn't the residue of a fire lit for control, like the braziers in Victory Plaza. This was the dust of the earth itself, ground down by time and gravity. It was the ultimate verdict. She looked at the rusting saxophone and saw its transformation. It was no longer an instrument of pain, but a relic, an offering to this new place of worship. The individual scream had been subsumed into the collective amen.

A single, nervous guard came later, sent by the *Bureau of Counter Intelligence* to investigate "unauthorized gatherings." He stood on the rim, wrote down the number 8647 on his report, and watched. He saw no signs, heard no chants, saw no leaders. He saw people standing silently, listening to birds. What was the crime? What was the subversion? He could find no words to describe it, and the BCI had no category for it. He left, frustrated, his report reading only: "Citizens observing local wildlife. No actionable dissent detected."

The power of the quarry was its passive resistance. The regime knew how to fight an enemy it could see. It did not know how to fight a sound, or a feeling, or a place. As the sun set and the stars emerged, brighter here away from the city's meager lights, the people slowly left. But they carried the hum back with them, not just in their memories, but in their bodies. The quarry's amen was now a part of the city's heartbeat, a deep, steady pulse beneath the crumbling pavement, a silent, vibrating promise that they were not just resisting—they were returning to something older and stronger than any Leader.

Chapter 3

Victory Plaza stretched out in all directions as a vast expanse of empty stone paving that seemed to swallow sound and movement alike. Creating an atmosphere of unnatural stillness in the heart of the city. At the very center of this empty space stood the bronze statue of the Leader that had been erected during the height of his power. A larger-than-life representation with one arm raised and hand open in a gesture that could be interpreted as either blessing or command. The statue showed clear signs of neglect and natural processes taking their course, with a green patina coating the bronze surface and moss growing thick in the folds of the sculpted coat and the crevices of the ear. This organic growth climbed steadily up the legs of the statue as if claiming the human form for the earth from which it had come.

A young woman stood at the base of the statue with a clipboard in her hands. Her practical clothing and tied-back hair suggested she was there for work rather than contemplation or protest. She was a biology student engaged in a methodical study of the statue's deterioration. She measured the cracks that had begun to appear in the bronze surface with clinical precision. She used a fine caliper to measure a hairline fracture that ran from the statue's heel up its calf, noting the measurement on her clipboard before moving to the next crack with complete absorption in her task. This was not an act of vandalism or political statement but simply an act of objective observation and recording of verifiable facts.

Mira watched from a stone bench at the edge of the plaza, noting the student's focus and lack of emotional investment in what she was documenting. The student stepped back from the statue to look up at the moss coverage. Making another note on her clipboard before speaking her conclusions in a low clinical voice that carried in the quiet space. She stated that the structural integrity had been compromised by moisture penetration accelerating internal corrosion, with moss roots exacerbating surface fractures in a predictable pattern of decay. She calculated that eventual failure would occur within fifteen to twenty years, perhaps sooner if freeze-thaw cycles continued at their current rate.

This dispassionate verdict felt like a sentence being passed by nature itself. Delivered without malice or hope but simply as a statement of inevitable fact. Mira's eyes moved to the base of the statue where the marble inscription had been altered by biological processes rather than human intervention. The original words "*FOR THE PEOPLE*" had been transformed by the acidic quality of pigeon droppings that had etched away parts of certain letters, changing the message to "*FOR THE PIGEONS*" through a slow natural editing process. This was not vandalism but a correction performed by the very creatures the plaza had been designed to exclude.

Mrs. Nova walked into the plaza with her eyes initially on the ground before looking up to take in the transformed statue and its altered inscription. She read the new words several times as if confirming what she was seeing. A sharp exhalation escaping her that was not quite a laugh but more a release of long-held tension. The sound represented surprise and recognition and absurdity all at once. Easing the tension in her shoulders just slightly as she absorbed the meaning of this transformation. Mira stood and walked to the base of the statue, ignoring the towering figure above to focus on the marble and moss at its foot.

She took a small glass vial from her bag and used a spoon to scrape up a sample of the white marble dust mixed with fragments of green moss, sealing and labeling it as verdict residue before adding it to her growing collection. The biology student packed her caliper away and left the plaza now that her work was complete and the facts had been properly recorded. Mrs. Nova stood for another moment looking at the words before shaking her head and walking away. Leaving Mira alone with the decaying statue that seemed smaller now that its inevitable fate had been documented. The guards would come later to check the plaza and note the changes in reports, but the reports could not stop what had already been set in motion by natural processes that answered to no human authority.

The statue continued to stand in the empty plaza but now seemed to be waiting rather than dominating. Its surface slowly being eaten and edited by forces that had no interest in human concepts of power or permanence. The erosion would continue day by day and crack by crack regardless of who noticed or documented it, a process that would eventually yield to the sentence that had been passed by the impartial judge of time and nature. The pigeons would continue to roost on the outstretched arm and contribute their own amendments to the inscription below. Their presence becoming increasingly appropriate as the original meaning of the monument faded into biological fact. The marble dust at the base would continue to accumulate as the stone yielded to weather and time. Creating new residue for anyone who thought to collect it as evidence of what happens to all human constructions eventually.

The decay of the statue was a microcosm of the decay infecting the entire regime. The Bureau of Belligerent Blunder Heads, in a final, fitting act of incompetence, issued a directive about the "patriotic maintenance of public monuments." They allocated funds for cleaning and repairs, but the funds were siphoned off by mid-level functionaries for their own use, and the work was never done. The statue continued to green, the cracks continued to spread. Their bluster had become background noise, the irritable buzzing of a fly trapped behind glass.

The Bureau of Counter Intelligence understood the symbolism all too well. They saw the biological student's report—filed, of course, under ID #8647—and recognized its terrifying implication. The report wasn't seditious; it was just *true*. And truth was the one thing their entire apparatus could not withstand. They could arrest a person for humming, but they could not arrest moss for growing. They could rewrite a history book in the Hall of Historical Corrections, but they could not rewrite the chemical process of oxidation. Their power had always relied on the manipulation of human perception, and now they were faced with an opponent that had no perception to manipulate: nature itself.

Meanwhile, Mira's collection of residues had taken on a new meaning. The vial of marble dust and moss wasn't just about memory anymore; it was evidence in a trial where nature was the prosecutor and time was the judge. Her shelf of jars was no longer a memorial; it was a forensic archive documenting a collapse.

This stand-off between unassailable truth and flailing power was playing out across the city. The Library of Errors was now mostly deserted, its curators having quietly stopped coming to work. But across the city, a new, living library was being curated. The geranium on the steps had spawned others. Cuttings from it had been potted in tin cans and cracked teacups and were now blooming on windowsills throughout the district. The original press badge was now completely buried under a riot of roots and flowers. A secret heart feeding the vibrant green growth above.

This was the final, most profound act of The Undercurrent. They weren't just preserving the old world; they were actively gardening the new one. Rosa's seedpods, carefully planted in vacant lots and hidden corners, were sprouting. The "brown scriptures" were becoming green realities. The city was being slowly, patiently rewilded, not with forests, but with truth. A truth that grew, and breathed, and could not be contained in a glass case or burned in a furnace.

The statue in the plaza, with its new, pigeon-authored inscription, was no longer a monument to the Leader. It had been repurposed. It was now a monument to the absurdity of his ambition. A lesson in entropy, and a feeding station for birds. The regime had tried to etch its story in stone and bronze, but the wind and the rain and the pigeons were editing the text. And the new story they were writing was infinitely more interesting. Mrs. Nova's sharp exhalation of air, halfway between a laugh and a sob, was the perfect eulogy for the whole failed project. It was the sound of a spell being broken. The statue, like the regime it represented, was still standing). But everyone who passed it now could see it was just waiting to fall.

Chapter 4

The landfill stretched toward the horizon as a vast landscape of everything the city had thrown away and tried to forget. Hills of broken appliances and valleys of shredded plastic creating an artificial topography of abandonment. The air carried a complex smell of rot and chemicals that created a sharp sweet odor of decay which hung over everything like an invisible cloud. Mira walked along the narrow paths that wound between these piles of discarded objects. Her eyes scanning the ground without specific purpose but taking in everything she saw. This place represented the city's unwanted memory, the physical evidence of all that had been deemed no longer useful or desirable by the society that had created it.

A sudden flash of color different from the surrounding plastic caught her attention, revealing itself as a paper postcard half-buried in a mound of food scraps and torn fabric. The postcard remained surprisingly clean with sharp edges despite its surroundings. A picture of a perfect beach with blue water and white sand that seemed utterly disconnected from this place of waste. Something green was growing from the center of the postcard, a small determined shoot that had pushed through the paper and broken the image of the ideal beach. Mira bent down to look more closely without touching the fragile object, reading the faded but clear writing on the reverse side of the card.

The message expressed missing someone and a promise to be home soon. Signed with a child's name that suggested a message of hope sent to someone who was probably gone now. This communication had been thrown away like everything else here, but the paper had held a seed that decided to grow despite the circumstances. On the edge of the massive landfill there existed a small settlement of huts constructed from scrap wood and metal sheeting, where people survived by foraging through what the city had discarded. A young girl named Anya lived in one of these makeshift structures with quick hands and observant eyes that missed nothing valuable in the waste.

She found a spent bullet casing in the dirt near her hut, its brass material still cool to the touch even in the sunlight. She wiped away the dirt to reveal the metallic surface beneath. Then noticed a wilted seedling growing near a leaky water pipe that seemed unlikely to survive much longer in the open. She took the bullet casing and filled it with damp soil from beside the pipe. Carefully lifting the fragile seedling with its thread-like roots to place it in this new container. She pressed the soil gently around the base of the plant and put the casing on her windowsill where the afternoon sun could reach it, watering it each day with a few drops from her drinking cup.

The plant did not die as might have been expected but instead grew stronger. With leaves turning a deeper green until it put out a bud that eventually opened. The flower glowed with a soft violet light in the dim interior of the hut, creating a beautiful contrast to its rough surroundings. At dusk each day the flower began to produce a low pure hum that filled the small space with a sustained sound of life and defiance against all expectations. Anya named the plant Tuesday after the day she had found it, forming a connection that went beyond simple categorization or usefulness.

She took the plant to the single-room school where a tired teacher instructed students from old books containing only approved facts. Anya showed the teacher the flower in its bullet casing home, expecting some recognition of this small miracle she had nurtured. The teacher looked at the plant without smiling and declared it a weed with a scientific name that meant nothing to the girl, stating it had no use because it bore no fruit and could not be eaten. She called the flower a distraction from more important matters and told Anya to put it away during class time.

Anya held the plant in her lap instead of putting it away, feeling the gentle hum through her fingers as a truth that existed outside official categories and permissions. This thing was useless by the teacher's standards but beautiful and persistent and defiant in its own right, requiring no justification beyond its own existence. She would continue to nurture it regardless of the dismissal from authority. Recognizing the hum as her personal truth that needed no validation.

The sound continued each dusk as a quiet but undeniable presence in the settlement. A vibration that seemed to resonate with something fundamental in the world beyond human constructions of value and usefulness. The flower thrived in its bullet casing home without concern for how it was categorized or dismissed. Simply continuing its cycle of growth and sound production as it had evolved to do. Anya watched over it with a protective attention that needed no explanation or justification. Understanding something that the teacher with her approved facts could not seem to grasp. The hum spread through the settlement each evening as a reminder that some truths operated outside the systems humans created to control and categorize their world.

The bullet casing continued to serve as an adequate container for the growing plant. Its original purpose transformed into something entirely different through this unexpected adoption. The settlement continued to exist on the edge of the landfill, drawing sustenance from what others had thrown away while creating meaning from what they found valuable. The teacher continued to teach from the old books with their approved facts, perhaps never understanding what she had dismissed that day in her classroom. The flower continued to hum each dusk. Its sound joining the other small persistent notes that were emerging throughout the city as things continued to unravel and reform in new configurations.

The landfill settlement was more than a shantytown; it was a living critique of the regime's entire philosophy. While the Bureau of Belligerent Blunder Heads preached about economic productivity and the Hall of Historical Corrections curated a past of glorious industry, the people here were building a life from the regime's waste. They had created a thriving, informal economy based on repair, reuse, and rediscovery. A man named Leo, who had once been an engineer before being declared "ideologically unsound," now ran a workshop where he brought broken machinery back to life. Not for profit, but for the sheer, defiant joy of making something work again.

This economy of repair was the absolute opposite of the Library of Errors. The Library was a place of static, false information. The landfill was a place of dynamic, rediscovered truth. A child here could tell you the real tensile strength of salvaged wire. The true nutritional value of a root foraged from the contaminated soil. Or, the actual way to patch a roof to keep out the rain. Their knowledge was earned, tested, and practical. It was a knowledge that could not be found in any book approved by the Bureau of Counter Intelligence.

Anya's flower, humming in its bullet-casing pot, became a symbol of this entire economy. It was value created from nothing, beauty forged from neglect, truth spoken in a frequency the powerful were deaf to. The BCI agent who eventually came to investigate the settlement—drawn by rumors of "unsanctioned communal living"—walked right past it. He saw only squalor and disorder. He filed his report, noting the "marginalization of approved educational standards" and the "potential for unregulated resource accumulation." He completely missed the flower on the windowsill, its soft violet light, its gentle hum. He had no category for it. It was, as the teacher had said, useless. And therefore, beneath his notice.

This was the great blind spot of the regime. It could only understand value in terms of what it could control, tax, and weaponize. The flower's hum was a dividend that paid out in a currency of spirit. A currency they had long ago abolished. Mira, walking among the shacks, understood this. She saw Leo's workshop and recognized it as a sister endeavor to the Institution of Heretical Science—a place where the real, physical truth of the world was respected and understood. She traded a pair of warm socks for a beautifully rewired lamp. In that transaction, she felt more genuine economic activity than in a year of the state's managed rations and production quotas.

As she left the settlement, the hum of Anya's flower followed her, a quiet, persistent signal. It was the same note from the quarry, from the basement, from the hum that had spread through the city. It was all connected. The Undercurrent wasn't a political movement; it was an ecological one. It was the natural response of life to a system that sought to sterilize and control. It found the cracks, it planted seeds, and it grew, regardless of permission. The regime was trying to hold back the ocean with a strainer. In a small hut on the edge of a mountain of trash, a little girl and her flower were proof that the tide was already coming in.

Chapter 5

The regime did not fall in any dramatic or violent fashion but simply stopped functioning one day, as if those performing it had collectively decided to cease their roles. The checkpoints stood empty without explanation. The gray uniforms disappeared from the streets as though they had never been there at all. The loudspeakers that had once filled the air with constant announcements fell silent, creating a void where the expected sounds of control should have been. There was no official announcement or victory parade to mark this change, just a gradual realization that the machinery had ceased to operate. The city held its breath in this strange absence, waiting for some sound or signal that never came to explain what was happening.

Mira went to the riverbank carrying the bag that had become heavy with all the residues she had collected as evidence of the collapsing world. She stood looking at the water that moved past with its steady indifferent flow, then opened the bag without looking inside at its contents. She turned it over and shook out everything she had gathered—the river mud and quarry dust, the ash-soil and marble powder with moss—into the waiting current. The materials swirled and dissolved and vanished into the larger body of water that would carry them all to the sea, erasing the physical proof of both loss and persistence that she had so carefully preserved.

She was left holding only the empty bag and the single jar with its blood smear from that day in November. She waded into the water to submerge the jar completely. The river water filled the container and swirled behind the glass, blurring the dark red mark that had represented her vow of remembrance. She sealed the jar and held it up to the light, no longer a vessel for ash but now a container of the ever-moving present that was constantly renewing itself. This transformation felt like an acceptance that the ache itself was what mattered rather than any physical evidence she could preserve.

Rosa found the foraging girl working among the plants in the botanical gardens, digging for roots with her practiced hands. She approached with the second seedpod that contained the longer undeciphered message, asking if the girl could read its meaning. The girl took the pod and traced the bumps with her fingers, moving slowly with concentrated attention to the patterns. She announced that it contained just one long word, her fingers stopping as she spoke the word "*PERSIST*" as both declaration and instruction.

Rosa took the pod back and found a patch of soft earth between the roots of a large tree. Digging a small hole with her finger to place the pod inside. She covered it with soil without speaking any words, understanding that the message was now in the ground where it would do its work in silence. This action represented the true nature of change as she had come to understand it—not a single dramatic event but a collection of small stubborn acts that accumulated over time. Mrs. Nova stealing a shard of glass and a student measuring cracks in a statue were part of this pattern, along with a girl planting a badge under a geranium and another nurturing a humming flower.

The sum of these actions created a persistent quiet truth that ultimately outlasted all the shouting and grand declarations of power.

On a wall near one of the empty checkpoints a new poster appeared with different colors and slogans and a new face smiling with confidence. Suggesting the cycle was already resetting itself with different machinery. In a small apartment a woman watered a plant on her windowsill that hummed its soft steady note, filling the room with a sound that was useless by official standards but beautiful in its persistence.

The river continued its endless flow to the sea while the seed in the garden pushed a green shoot toward the sun, representing the continuous cyclical life that operated beyond human political systems. The ache for memory and the defiance of erasure revealed themselves as the permanent state of being alive rather than problems to be solved. This holy ache would outlive all flags and leaders and lies, humming on into whatever uncertain future awaited with its quiet endless note that asked only to be remembered. The paperwork that would document this transition period would be assigned numbers including 8647, but these numbers would have no more power over what was growing and flowing and persisting than they had over the previous regime that had faded away.

The Library of Errors remained standing with its shelves of wrong information, waiting for someone to decide what to do with all that accumulated falsehood. The Cathedral of Silence continued to stand with its damaged eye still reading *"ALMOST FREE"* to anyone who bothered to look up. The Hall of Historical Correction remained closed with its displays of condemned objects, their warnings now meaningless without anyone to enforce them. All these places would likely be renamed and repurposed in time, but for now they stood as monuments to a performance that had simply stopped one day without ceremony or explanation.

The girl in the settlement continued to care for the flower she named Tuesday. The hum joining with other small sounds throughout the city that were creating a new kind of music. The biology student continued her measurements of decay wherever she found it interesting to document, her caliper recording facts without concern for their meaning. The backpacker continued his journey along the riverbank, performing small rituals of reconciliation where they felt needed. Mrs. Nova kept her shard of glass in a small box by her bed, taking it out sometimes to feel its sharp edges and remember that she had diminished the gaze that once judged her.

All of them carried the holy ache in their own way, understanding that this was the human condition that no regime could ever eliminate or satisfy completely. The new posters would continue to appear with new faces and new slogans. But, the river would continue to flow and the seeds would continue to grow. And, the flowers would continue to hum regardless of what was promised or threatened. The ache would persist because it was not something that could be buried or erased, only acknowledged and carried forward into whatever came next. This was the permanent truth that outlasted all temporary arrangements of power. The endless note that would continue long after all the speeches had faded into silence.

The end was not an explosion, but an exhalation. The Bureau of Belligerent Blunder Heads simply stopped blundering because there was no one left to demand their performative loyalty. The Bureau of Counter Intelligence found itself with nothing to counter, its agents fading back into the population, their file numbers, including 8647, becoming meaningless digits in abandoned databases. The Light House went dark, its generators falling silent. Its spotlights extinguished, allowing the natural darkness of the coast to return for the first time in decades. The regime didn't collapse; it atrophied. It forgot how to be, because the people had forgotten how to fear it.

Mira's act at the river was the final, necessary unbinding. The ashes she had collected were the residue of a specific, terrible time. By returning them to the water, she was not forgetting. She was choosing a different way to remember. She was trading the weight of evidence for the flow of time. The jar of river water with its blurred blood-smear was a far more potent relic; it was a captured moment of the world moving on, a tiny ecosystem of renewal.

In the days that followed, the city began to breathe differently. The air itself seemed clearer without the constant odor of fear. The

Tower of Song remained, its melodies now blending with the sounds of children playing in streets they had previously hurried down. The *Jazz Club* opened its doors wide, and the music that spilled out was no longer a clandestine act of defiance but a public celebration of sound for its own sake.

Rosa's planted seedpod did more than just persist. It germinated, and the tree that grew from it became known for the strange, bumpy texture of its bark. Children would run their hands over it, unconsciously tracing the word their grandparents had fought to remember. The *Institution of Heretical Science* quietly dropped the "Heretical" from its name, its scientists emerging from isolation to help repair the city's crumbling infrastructure with actual, tested knowledge.

The *Undercurrent* did not declare victory. It had never been an organization that could hold a meeting or give a speech. It had been a frequency, a pattern of connection. And now that its purpose was achieved, it simply dissolved back into the population, its work done. Its members were just people now—a woman who could map the city's veins from memory, a girl who nurtured humming flowers, a man who remembered how to fix broken things.

The new posters on the walls were a warning of a cycle Mira understood all too well. But the ache she carried was no longer a wound; it was a compass. It was the understanding that the work was never finished. That freedom was not a state to be achieved but a practice to be maintained. A constant, gentle pressure against the tide of forgetting and the lure of easy lies.

That night, as the first stars appeared over the city, the hum could still be heard. It came from a thousand windowsills. From the rustle of leaves on a special tree. From the distant quarry. And, from the very soil itself. It was not a note of triumph, but one of vigilance. It was the sound of the world, patiently, persistently, remembering itself. And in her small apartment, listening to the quiet hum of her city, Mira finally understood the holy ache of the unbecoming. It was the price of staying human, and it was a price she would never stop paying.

The Silent Storm

Mira stood before the gray concrete building, the words Bureau of Belligerent Blunder Heads etched into the stone. She pushed the heavy door open. The man behind the counter did not look up. His uniform was crisp, his face blank. She stated her purpose for the seventh time. *Her son—The river—January*. He slid a familiar file across the counter. It was thin. The word *RUNAWAY* was stamped on the cover in red ink.

She did not accept it. She spoke of his freckle, his laugh, the tooth he lost at school. She described the packed lunch he never got to eat. The man's eyes glazed over with indifference. He recited the verdict. "Runaway. Accidental drowning. Case closed." His voice was a flat, practiced monotone. Mira's hands gripped the counter's edge. She demanded names, evidence, a reason. He said there was no reason to question the findings. The door behind him opened, and two larger men emerged. They stood, silent and imposing. The man behind the counter slid the file back into a drawer. The conversation was over.

She walked out into the damp city air. The Tower of Song dominated the skyline, its haunting melody weaving through the streets. The sound usually felt like a mockery, but today it sounded like a dirge. She passed the Cathedral of Silence, its doors sealed, absorbing every cry that was ever meant to be heard inside. She looked toward the Institution of Heretical Science, its windows dark. They had the answers, she was sure of it. They knew how the world really worked. But its doors were barred to people like her.

Back in her apartment, the silence was complete—suffocating. The music from the tower was just a faint vibration through the glass. She looked at his empty chair. She replayed every word from the Bureau, searching for a crack in their story, a hint of doubt. She found nothing. Their certainty was a solid wall—she wondered who paid for that wall. Her—Ben—Everyone who dissented.

She sat on the floor and pulled her knees to her chest. A dry sob escaped her, then another. The tears came then, hot and relentless. They were not gentle. They were a violent, silent storm that shook her entire body. She cried for the unanswered questions. She cried for the justice that would never come. She cried until her throat was raw and her eyes burned. The room darkened around her. She was completely alone. The city outside continued its slow decay, indifferent to the woman shattered at its core.

Without a Sound

The van doors opened to a deeper darkness. The Compliance Officers hauled him out, his boots scraping on stone. Before him, the Cathedral of Silence rose, a black stain against the night sky. In the distance, the Tower of Song glowed, its haunting melody a taunt he could no longer hear. They pushed him inside.

The silence hit him first. It was not an absence of noise, but a presence of its own. It pressed against his eardrums, refusing to allow any sound through. The vast space swallowed the sounds of their footsteps, their breathing, the rustle of their uniforms. Light from high, weak fixtures struggled to push back the gloom, creating small pools that ended abruptly in nothingness. On giant monitors mounted on the pillars, the Leader smiled. He addressed a rapt crowd, his mouth moving in a perfect, silent oration. White subtitles ghosted across the bottom of the screen, extolling unity and strength.

They did not speak—There words were of no use here. One officer held him while the other swung a fist. The impact against his jaw was a solid, jarring thud he felt in his teeth. The sound died the moment it was born. He cried out. His own voice was a vacuum in his head, a desperate strain in his throat that produced nothing. He saw his spit and blood float for a moment in the air before it splattered silently on the stone floor.

The beating was methodical. They worked with the bored efficiency of men performing a mundane task. A boot connected with his ribs. He felt the crack, a sharp, internal snap that stole his breath. He screamed again, a raw, tearing effort that the Cathedral consumed without a trace. His agony was a private event, witnessed only by the silent, smiling Leader on the screens.

They stopped. One officer held a document before his swollen eyes. On it was a pre-written confession. It detailed crimes of seditious thought, work record discrepancies, and negative influence. He shook his head, a slow, painful movement. The officer's face showed no reaction. He nodded to his partner.

The next phase began. They used tools now. A short, heavy club. The blows were precise, aimed at his joints, his kidneys, the base of his spine. Each impact was a seismic event in his body that the world would never hear. He tried to beg. He formed the words with his broken mouth. His wife's name was just a shape on his lips, a ghost without a sound. He saw only his own reflection, distorted and bloody, in the dark lenses of their goggles.

They presented the document again. His vision blurred. He could not focus on the words. He knew the choice was not between signing and not signing. It was between signing now or signing later, after more of this silent, infinite pain. His hand trembled violently as one officer forced a pen into his hand. He left a smudge of blood next to his signature.

The officers stepped back, their job was complete. They turned and walked away, their figures dissolving into the shadows without a single footfall. Tomasz was alone in the immense silence.

He lay on the cold stone floor. The monitors above him flickered, showing the Leader waving to an adoring crowd. Tomasz's breath came in shallow, ragged gasps. He felt a deep cold spreading from his core. He thought of the receipt they had given his wife. A transaction slip for a human life. He wondered if she would ever know the truth.

The darkness at the edges of his vision deepened, merging with the darkness of the Cathedral. The last thing he saw was the Leader's face, smiling its silent, perfect smile. Then, nothing. His body relaxed into a final stillness.

The Officers returned an hour later. They found him there. They checked for a pulse and found none. They exchanged a look that needed no sound. They picked him up, one under each arm, and carried his body to a side door. They loaded him into a different van. There was no report filed. No investigation opened. His file was stamped with a single word: *CLARIFIED*. The van drove away, leaving the Cathedral to its perfect, endless silence.

Jenna's Unbecoming

The air in the lecture hall was a thick cloud of forced reverence and dust. On the wall-mounted screens, the Leader's face was frozen in a moment of his trademark bombast, his tie a slash of violent red against his perpetually tanned skin. Professor Halden, a man whose spirit seemed to have been ironed flat by decades of compliance, was dissecting the Leader's latest address—a triumphant declaration of a record harvest.

"Note the Leader's clarity," Halden droned, his voice devoid of any conviction that wasn't mandated. "He cuts through the noise of false narratives with the precision of a surgeon. Any suggestion of shortage is *fake news*, a poison crafted by liars and traitors to weaken our glorious nation."

Jenna's pen lay still on her blank notebook. She saw not the Leader's smug grin, but the grim figures she'd glimpsed on her father's secured terminal—the real reports of failed crops and famine in the northern provinces. Elias, her father, a respected journalist at the state-run *Daily Beacon*, had gotten sloppy, leaving the data exposed for a single, devastating moment. That glimpse had shattered her last illusion about him. He wasn't a seeker of truth—not any more; he was now just a scribe for the regime, polishing its lies into something palatable.

Her gaze drifted from the screen to the wall beside the door. There, almost invisible amidst the scuffs and scratches, was a single, etched symbol: a gentle wave. Her heart gave a hard thump. It was the third one she'd seen that week. A secret sign in a world that permitted no secrets.

Later, in the stale-aired silence of her dorm, she pried up the loose floorboard by her bed. From the hollow space, she retrieved her own secret: a simple notebook. Every page was blank—except one.

On the first page, she had written a single line, a truth she hoped to one day show her father: *"The truth is a widow who outlives her eulogies."*

The wave symbol had led her to them, or they to her. They called themselves The Undercurrent. They were not an organization with a leader, but a movement—a collective of whispers, of shared glances, of people who knew the world was sick and were determined to heal it without violence. In the forgotten sub-basement of the library, between shelves of censored books, a sharp-faced boy from her logic class and an intense girl from the journalism lab had given her a purpose.

"They're erasing the famine," the girl had whispered, her eyes burning in the dim light. "The Bureau is scrubbing the data. We need someone to document the truth. To find the words for what's happening."

The assignment was treason. It was also the most honest work she had ever done. She collected stories—a murmured confession from a janitor from the north, the hollow-eyed fear of a kitchen worker whose family had vanished. She transcribed them in her tight, anxious script in a black-covered notebook, creating a record of the Leader's greatest lie. She painstakingly drew the Undercurrents wave symbol with silver ink on the cover.

The act of knowing the truth made it impossible to stay silent. It was a pressure in her chest, demanding release.

It happened in Halden's next lecture. He was replaying the harvest speech, his voice dripping with sycophantic praise. "To even question this victory is seditionist revisionism," he declared, parroting the state's favorite term for thoughtcrime.

Jenna's voice cut through the stifling air, calm and clear. "If the distribution networks were so efficient," she asked, "why did the initial internal reports from the northern commissars request emergency aid? Why were those requests classified?"

The silence was instantaneous and absolute. It was the sound of pure terror. Halden's face drained of color, not in anger, but in sheer panic at being associated with her contamination. He didn't answer. He simply stared, his mouth a small, round 'o' of horror, before gathering his notes and almost fleeing the room.

The judgment was not slow in coming.

She was summoned to a "disciplinary hearing." The room contained three university deans, a man from the Bureau of Counter Intelligence—and a representative from the Bureau of Belligerent Blunder Heads. The BCI man had the cold, empty eyes of a shark. The other—just empty.

There was no debate, no defense. Her question was entered into the record as evidence of "seditionist revisionism aimed at undermining the supreme authority of the Leader." The hearing was a formality, a piece of bureaucratic theater designed to lend a gloss of legitimacy to a predetermined outcome.

"Jenna Sharpe," the head dean said, not meeting her eyes, "you are expelled. Permanently. Your academic privileges are hereby revoked. You will be escorted to gather your belongings and removed from campus."

The security detail watched as she packed her life into a single duffel bag. Her hands were steady, her movements robotic. As she bent to retrieve a sweater from under her bed, her fingers found the loose floorboard. In one fluid motion, she slipped the notebook out and into the bag, burying it under clothes. The guards, either uninterested or oblivious to the significance of a student's journal, didn't notice.

The walk to the university's main gate was the longest of her life. The manicured lawns, the imposing lecture halls, the ever-present hum from the Tower of Song—it all looked the same, but she was now irrevocably outside of it.

The wrought-iron gates clanged shut behind her with a finality that echoed in her bones. She stood on the pavement, a single bag at her feet. She was no longer a student. She was an exile. A dissident.

But in her bag, wrapped in a sweater, was a notebook. A widow waiting for her time to speak. Jenna adjusted the strap on her shoulder, turned her back on the university, and walked into the city. Toward her parents house. Toward the whispering embrace of The Undercurrent. Her education was over. Her unbecoming had just begun.

The Leader of Victory Plaza

Polard Mundt slammed his textbook shut with a sound like a gunshot in the quiet library. The student across from him flinched, looking up from her notes with wide, startled eyes. Polard did not look at her. He stared out the tall leaded window at the spires of the city, his expression one of profound boredom laced with contempt. The Institution of Science dominated the view, a cold, granite monument to reason and order. He hated it.

He stood up, his chair scraping harshly against the stone floor. He gathered his things, not bothering to organize the expensive pens and leather-bound notebooks, and turned to leave. His elbow caught the edge of the girl's stack of books, sending them crashing to the floor. She gasped, scrambling to collect the scattered pages. Polard walked past her without a word, without a glance. The needs of others were a distant, irrelevant noise, a static he had long learned to tune out. His family's wealth was a buffer against consequence, a wall that separated him from the common people.

His footsteps echoed in the cavernous hallway. Other students gave him a wide berth, a mixture of fear and fascination in their glances. He cultivated this reaction. He wore his disdain like a fine suit. He believed the university, like the government it served, was a rotting edifice. He spent his nights not studying, but scouring obscure forums on the data-nets, falling down rabbit holes of conspiracy and grievance. He read about secret pacts and hidden agendas, about a deep state cabal he believed was systematically weakening the nation. He consumed these theories with a fervent, unquestioning hunger. They confirmed his own innate sense of superiority and his belief that the world was too stupid to see the obvious truth he saw.

He started talking about these ideas in the dining halls and common rooms. At first, people laughed. They dismissed him as the spoiled son of a wealthy industrialist, a boy playing at rebellion. But his conviction was absolute. He spoke with a blunt, shocking certainty that cut through the nuanced, careful language of his professors. He called the Institution of Science the Institution of Heretical Science. He said they poisoned the water and the air with their chemicals. He said they lied about the weather. He said they created plagues in their labs to control the population. His voice, loud and insistent, found a receptive audience among other disaffected, directionless children of privilege.

A man named Corbin sought him out after one such rant in a smoke-filled club. Corbin was older, with a sharp, calculating face and cheap suit. He bought Polard a drink and leaned in close. He told Polard his ideas were not just right, they were powerful. He said the people were hungry for a message that was not weak, not complicated, not academic. They wanted someone to blame. They wanted simple answers to complex problems. They wanted to feel strong again. Corbin had a group of like-minded individuals, men who saw the coming shift in the political winds. They needed a vessel for their ideas, a face. They wanted Polard.

Polard laughed at first. Politics was a dirty game for compromise and cowards. He had no desire to stand on a stage with those fools and beg for votes. He could say what he wanted from the sidelines, a critic untouched by the mess of governance. Corbin was persistent. He met with Polard again and again. He showed him polls and data. He explained how sentiment was turning against the old guard. He flattered Polard's ego, calling him a visionary, a prophet untainted by the system he sought to destroy. He said a real man did not criticize from the outside. A real man took charge and fixed the problems himself.

The flattery worked. The idea of power, real power, began to seduce Polard. It was not about service. It was about control. It was about proving his theories right and making everyone who had ever doubted him bow down. He agreed to run for president. His campaign was a spectacle. He rented large halls instead of using community centers. He bypassed the traditional media, speaking directly to the crowds through loudspeakers. His speeches were not policy discussions. They were rallies. They were performances.

He stood at a podium, his face flushed with a strange energy, his voice amplified to a deafening roar. He pointed a thick finger toward the Tower of Song in the distance. "They want to fill your heads with their weak melodies. They want to make you soft. They want you to forget the great songs of our past, the songs of strength." He gestured vaguely toward the Cathedral of Silence. "They want you to be quiet. They want you to obey. They do not want you to hear the truth. The truth is not quiet. The truth is loud."

He saved his most venomous rhetoric for the Institution of Science. "A nest of traitors and heretics. They sit in their tall tower and they look down on you. They think you are stupid. They think they can tell you anything. They say the sky is blue. Do you believe them? I do not believe them. They are liars. They are the worst kind of liars. They lie with numbers and charts. They want to confuse you. I will not let them confuse you."

As his poll numbers solidified, his rhetoric grew darker and more personal. He began to openly insult his opponents, calling them "weak-minded fools," "pathetic losers," and "puppets of the deep state." He turned his rallies into rituals of public contempt. "Look at them," he'd sneer. "They can't win on their ideas—they have no ideas! They have no passion! They have only their cheating, their lies, their plots to steal this election from you!" Night after night, he conditioned his followers. "The only way we can lose," he would thunder, jabbing a finger at the crowd, "is if it's rigged. Remember that. If I don't win, it's because they cheated. They are thieves and traitors, and they will try to rob you of your future!"

The crowds cheered. They screamed his name. They believed every word.

He never explained how he would fix anything. He only stated what was wrong and who was to blame. His sentences were short. His concepts were simple. He repeated himself constantly, hammering the same phrases into the collective consciousness until they became accepted facts. He spoke about enormous, impossible things, and he spoke about them with the casual certainty of a man discussing the weather. "We will build a great wall. We will make them pay for it. We will win so much you will be tired of winning." He began to promise a final, permanent solution. "This is the last election you will ever have to worry about," he vowed. "When we win, we will fix this broken system forever. You will have your victory, and you will never have to vote again. I will take care of everything." The people clung to him. They developed a cult-like fervor. At his rallies, they sold shirts with his face on them. They chanted his name in unison. They saw in him a reflection of their own anger, amplified and given permission to erupt.

Not everyone was swayed. A small group, journalists from independent papers, academics from the very institution he maligned, and ordinary citizens who saw the danger, tried to speak out. They wrote articles fact-checking his wild claims. They held counter-demonstrations. They warned about the rise of demagoguery. Their voices were drowned out by the roaring tide of his movement. He called them enemies of the people. He said they were part of the conspiracy. His followers turned on the dissenters with a viciousness that was terrifying. The election neared. The polls predicted a landslide. The energy in the city was electric, a current of pure, undiluted anticipation.

Election day was a formality. The results came in quickly, a tidal wave of victory. His supporters poured into the streets, chanting, crying, celebrating their deliverance. The central gathering point was Unity Plaza, a vast public space flanked by the city's oldest monuments. The old fountain, a popular spot for children, was ignored now. The crowd was a single, pulsing organism, their faces turned toward a large stage erected at the far end. The air hummed with a low, expectant roar.

Polard Mundt stood in the wings of the stage, watching them. He felt nothing for them, these faceless, adoring masses. They were a means to an end. They were the engine of his will. He smoothed down his dark suit. He did not sweat. His posture was unnaturally straight.

He walked onto the stage. The roar that greeted him was physical, a wall of sound that hit him in the chest. He stood at the microphone, letting the adulation wash over him. He held up his hands for silence. The crowd obeyed instantly, the noise dropping to a hushed, reverent whisper.

He leaned into the microphone. His voice was calm, a hypnotic monotone that carried to the very edges of the plaza. "Thank you. Thank you. This is a great victory. A tremendous victory. The greatest victory this nation has ever seen. You have done this. You, the people, have spoken. You have told the liars and the cheats and the heretics that we will not take it anymore. We are taking our nation back."

"They tried to cheat," he stated, his voice dropping to a conspiratorial whisper that forced the crowd to lean in. "Oh, they tried. But you were too many. Your will was too strong. They could not steal what was so clearly, so rightfully ours!" The crowd roared its defiance. He nodded, a grim smile on his face. "But we have won. And this victory is just the beginning. I promised you that if we won, we would fix things. We will fix them forever. The chaos of the past is over. The endless, pointless arguing is over. You will never have to be troubled by the farce of another election again. I will be your voice. Now and always."

He paused, letting the cheers rise and fall. He looked out at the sea of faces, at the flags with his name waving frantically. "They think we are a movement. They are wrong. We are a revolution. They think I am a candidate. They are wrong. From this moment forward, I am not a candidate. I am not a president. I am not Polard Mundt. That name is a relic. It belongs to the past. A weak past. A past of compromise. That past is over."

He let the silence hang, thick and heavy. The crowd was utterly still, hanging on his every word. "You need a title that means something. A title that shows strength. A title that shows victory. You will call me something new. You will call me The Leader. Say it with me. The Leader." The crowd erupted. "The Leader! The Leader! The Leader.!" The chant became a mantra, a prayer, a weapon.

He nodded, a small, cold smile crossing his lips. He pointed to the ground beneath their feet. "And this place. This place where we stand. They call it Unity Plaza. Unity." He said the word like it was a curse. "A weak word. A passive concept. A relic of a compromising past. We do not believe in unity with our enemies. We believe in victory over our enemies. Victory." He slammed his fist on the podium. "Victory is active. Victory is decisive. Victory belongs to us. To you and to me. From this moment on, this sacred ground will have a new name. It will be called Victory Plaza. Let the world remember this night. Let them remember that this is where victory began. This is where the new world began. This is where I, your Leader, began." The crowd screamed its approval, a sound of pure, unthinking devotion that echoed off the cold stone of the surrounding buildings, a sound that promised to drown out everything else forever.

The Holy and the Broken

The ache began not in the ears, but in the mind. For Rosa, it was a physical pull, a tide in the blood that turned her face, always, toward the city's heart. The Tower of Song was a pale, needle-like spire piercing the perpetually gray sky, and from it, the music never ceased. It was the city's soundtrack and its siren call, a haunting, wordless melody that spoke of a loss so beautiful it could break a heart that hadn't already been shattered by the Republic. It was a *holy* sound, presented as a sacred gift, but it was built upon the *broken*.

Rosa's mother, Agata, had been taken for the songs she wove into coat linings. Her father had vanished years before for humming a tune that predated the Leader. Music was Rosa's inheritance and her curse. She heard the Tower's song more clearly than most; it was a symphony of all the stolen voices, a ghostly choir of the silenced, the musicians who had been tuned to the Republic's frequency or shattered for refusing. It was a *holy* choir built from *broken* people with broken hearts.

Since her mother's arrest, the song had changed. Woven into the ethereal, *holy* harmonies was a new thread, a specific, plaintive phrase played on what sounded like a glass armonica—her mother's favorite instrument. It was a sound of pure, crystalline grief, a *broken* note that was a hook in Rosa's soul, pulling her, day by day, closer to the pale tower.

She fought it. She was part of the Undercurrent now. Her rebellion was etching the humming sequence—remember, remember, remember—onto park benches and piping it through the steam vents in the street. But the Tower's *holy* melody was a constant counterpoint to her quiet work, a state-sponsored opiate meant to soothe the populace into a beautiful, mournful stupor. Yes, you are *broken*, it seemed to say. But isn't the breaking exquisite? It aestheticized their pain, made a sacrament of their suffering.

One evening, as a cold drizzle slickened the cobblestones, the pull became unbearable. The glassy phrase from the tower was her mother's signature, clear as a fingerprint. It wasn't just a memory; it felt like a summons from something both *holy* and profoundly *broken*. Elias, the journalist she sometimes shared a stolen moment of silence with, had warned her. "It's a trap, Rosa," he'd whispered, his voice raw from the furnace smoke of incinerated history. "They use what we love to bait the hook. They know you'll come for this *holy* lie."

But what if it wasn't? What if the rumor was true? What if the spirits of the lost musicians really were in there, and her mother was trying to communicate? The hope was a more potent lure than any fear.

She found herself at the edge of Victory Plaza, the vast, barren expanse that separated the city from the Tower. The Leader's giant face, projected onto a screen of mist, stared down, his sweatless visage a mockery of human effort. The Tower stood behind him, a thing of stark, elegant geometry. The *holy* song swelled, and the *broken* glass armonica line trilled, a needle of sound straight into Rosa's heart.

She took a step onto the plaza. Then another. The music folded around her, a welcoming embrace. It promised an end to the fighting, to the fear, to the *holy* ache of unbecoming that was resistance. It promised a reunion in harmony. She was halfway across the vast square, a solitary figure drawn toward the beautiful sound, when the music shifted.

It began to incorporate her. The soft tap of her boots on the wet stone became a percussive element. The quick, shallow rhythm of her breath was woven into the woodwind section. The Tower wasn't just playing to her; it was playing her. She was becoming a part of the performance, her living, *broken* fear and hope and love instrumented for the benefit of the silent, watching windows of the city. They were making her *brokenness holy*.

Panic cut through the trance. This was the trap. Not to kill her, but to assimilate her. To turn her very life into a beautiful, state

controlled elegy. Her resistance, her love for her mother, her grief—
all of it would be sanctified and added to the soundtrack, proof of the
Republic's generosity in allowing such beautiful sorrow to exist.

She would not be a *holy* note in their *broken* song. She would
facilitate the Tower's unbecoming.

Rosa did the only thing she could think of. She opened her
mouth, and she hummed. It was a weak, shaky, *broken* sound,
instantly swallowed by the Tower's majestic output. But she hummed
the sequence. The repeated three-note motif of the Undercurrent.
Remember—Remember—Remember.

She wasn't just humming it for herself. She was humming it
for the Tower. For the voices trapped inside. *Remember who you
were. Remember this is a cage.*

She took a step back. The *holy* music seemed to falter for a
fraction of a second, a needle scratch on a vast, ethereal record. In that
instant, she heard it—not the beautiful, homogenized harmony, but
the raw, discordant, truly *broken* cry of anguish that lay beneath it.
The true sound of imprisonment.

She took another step back, then another, each one a physical
tearing away from the magnetic pull. Her *broken* humming was her
anchor, a tiny, defiant lifeboat on a sea of manufactured *holiness*. She
hummed for her mother, for her father, for all the stolen. She hummed
until her throat was raw, her feet carrying her backward out of the
plaza.

When she finally broke free of its acoustic grip, leaning
against a sooty wall in a narrow alley, the Tower's song returned to its
default state of beautiful, haunting melancholy. It had resumed its
holy lie. But Rosa heard it differently now. She heard the prison bars
in the harmony, the *broken* despair in the crescendo.

She returned to her work that night with a new ferocity. She
didn't just etch the wave symbol; she etched small musical staves,

with the three-note sequence of the Undercurrent. She taught the children in the landfill community not just to hum, but to recognize the false *holiness* in the Tower's beauty, and the true power in their own *broken* anthem.

The Tower of Song still played. Its music was still hauntingly *holy*, and it still lured the grieving and the hopeful to their doom. But for Rosa, and for those she taught, it was no longer a mystery. It was the enemy's greatest weapon and its most glaring confession: a society that must enslave even the souls of its artists to pretend it has a heart, has none at all. And Rosa's own song, small and *broken* and defiant, became a counter-melody that would, in time, help the whole city hear the truth behind the beautiful lie.

The Final Clarification

Guard 8647 did not sweat. The heat in the furnace room was immense, a physical weight that pressed the cheap gray fabric of his uniform against his skin. But his brow remained dry. He watched the man, Elias, feed history into the flames. The dry pages blackened and vanished. 8647's job was to ensure the burning was complete. No fragments were to escape.

He saw it happen. A small charred scrap, caught in an updraft, twisted back and landed near the journalist's boot. The man almost kicked it into the fire. Then he stopped. He bent and picked it up. 8647 saw his eyes scan the surviving text. He saw the man's fingers tremble before he folded the paper and shoved it deep into his pocket.

8647 said nothing. He made a note in his mind. The infraction was minor. A single word, *"LIAR,"* on a scrap. But it was a seed. He had seen how seeds grew.

Later, he stood at the riverbank, partially concealed by a rusted barge. He watched the journalist. He saw the man pull the scrap from his pocket. The wind snatched it. 8647 watched the paper float on the oily water, the word *"LIAR"* facing the sky for a moment before it soaked through and sank. He made another mental note. The evidence was gone, but the thought was not. The man was compromised.

8647's life was a ledger of such notes. He was a scalpel for the body of the state, cutting away infection. The humming in the basement, the marks on the walls, the woman who collected ash. He filed them all under his internal number. He was efficient. He was necessary.

The order came directly from the Task Force. Elias was to be brought in for clarification. 8647 was assigned to the extraction team. They took the man from his apartment in the dead of night. He broke quickly. He gave them names, real and imagined. He gave them Rosa. 8647 recorded it all. The man's fear was a sour smell in the white room.

He was there for the raid on the button factory. He was the one who broke the water glasses. The sound of their destruction was clean, definitive. But then the humming started. It was a sound from their bodies. A sound he could not break. He had stood there, confused, his hand frozen in the air. He had filed the report. "Successful dispersal of a public nuisance." But the hum had followed him home. It echoed in the silent moments before sleep.

The system began to falter. The Leader was gone. The loudspeakers fell silent. The checkpoints stood empty. 8647's uniform felt like a costume. His purpose, his entire being, was tied to a machine that had stopped grinding.

He found himself walking. His feet carried him to the granite quarry. He stood on the rim and looked down at the people listening to the pigeons. He saw the rusted saxophone, the woman collecting dust. He felt the hum through the soles of his boots. He took out his notepad. "Citizens observing local wildlife," he wrote. The words were meaningless. He could find no category for this.

He saw her then. The woman from the plaza. Mira. She was standing with the music woman, Rosa. They looked at him. There was no fear in their eyes. Only a deep, weary recognition. They saw the number on his badge. They saw the empty man beneath it.

He turned and walked away, back toward the silent city. The Bureau was deserted. Dust coated the desks. On his superior's chair lay a single sheet of paper. A list. His name was on it. His number. 8647. The order was simple. "Clarification."

He understood. The tool was no longer needed. It was to be discarded. Purged from the record.

He did not run. He walked to the Cathedral of Silence. The great doors were unlocked. He stepped inside.

The silence was absolute. It was not an absence of sound, but a presence. It filled his ears, his mind, his lungs. He walked to the center of the vast space and stood there.

He waited.

The doors opened. Two figures entered. They wore the same gray uniform he did. Their faces were blank, professional. Their badges read 8651 and 8652.

They did not speak. They did not need to.

8647 looked at them. He saw himself in their empty eyes. He was not afraid. He finally understood the nature of the machine he served. It did not hate him. It felt nothing for him at all.

He closed his eyes as they approached. The last thing he heard was the sound of his own heartbeat, a frantic, lonely rhythm in the perfect, infinite silence. Then, nothing.

The Holy Ache of the Unbecoming

A Screenplay

Part I

EXT. VICTORY PLAZA - DAY

A vast concrete square, baking under a merciless sun. Heat shimmers distort the edges of decaying buildings. A dry fountain, filled with litter, stands as a centerpiece.

A dense CROWD stands motionless, a sea of gray and brown coats. The air is filled with suppressed energy and collective body heat.

Among them, MIRA (40's, eyes hollow with a grief she carries like a stone), shifts her weight. Her feet ache in worn-out shoes. Sweat traces a path down her neck.

Her hand is buried in her coat pocket, clutching a small, worn photograph. Her thumb moves rhythmically over its edge.

SOUNDS of a haunting, wordless ARIA weaving through the murmur of the crowd. Mira's eyes drift to the distant TOWER OF SONG piercing the hazy skyline.

Others subtly tilt their heads, listening. A shared moment of longing.

A CRACKLE of harsh static from loudspeakers. The Tower's melody is brutally drowned out by a pre-recorded FANFARE.

The crowd SHUFFLES forward as one. A wave of expectation builds.

Every head turns in unison toward an empty stage draped in banners of a single, solid color.

THE LEADER (POLARD MUNDT, 60's, but unnaturally smooth-faced, hair a dull, perfect helmet of sienna) steps into the light. Flanked by men in dark suits, their faces blank masks.

He raises his hands. Absolute silence falls.

                         THE LEADER
          People.

He lets the word hang, possessive.

                    THE LEADER (CONT'D)
          Look around you. See the decay? The weakness? A sickness
          of disorder choked us. A plague of indecision. That pathetic
          time is now officially finished.

A sharp, violent CHEER erupts. Fists punch the air.

                            CROWD
                      (Chanting, in unison)
             FINISHED! FINISHED! FINISHED!

Mira keeps her hands in her pockets. One on the photo, the other a hidden fist.

The Leader waits for the noise to die.

                         THE LEADER
          We must build anew. We demand strength. A single purpose.
          Real Change.

The crowd roars.

                            CROWD
                      (Chanting, in unison)
             CHANGE! CHANGE! CHANGE!

Mira watches the fervent faces, feeling nothing but a hollow, expanding dread.

BEGIN FLASHBACK

EXT. SUNNY PARK - DAY (FLASHBACK)

The sun is golden, not harsh. The world is in color. GREEN grass, BLUE sky.

A young boy, BEN (7, impossibly bright, gap-toothed smile), runs across the grass, his laughter pure and unfettered.

MIRA (years younger, face soft with joy) chases him. He darts behind a large OAK TREE.

                    MIRA
          I'm gonna get you, you little monster!

She creeps around the tree. Giggles from above. She looks up. Ben is perched on a low, thick branch, beaming down at her.

                    BEN
          I'm the king of the castle!

                    MIRA
          And I'm the dirty rascal!

She pulls herself up, sitting beside him. They swing their legs. He leans his head against her arm.

                    BEN
          What's that smell?

Mira inhales deeply. The air is sweet.

                    MIRA
          Honeysuckle. And cut grass. And...sunshine.

Ben scrunches his nose.

                    BEN
     Sunshine doesn't smell.

                    MIRA
     Everything good has a smell. You just have to know how to
     look for it.

She plucks a leaf, holds it to his nose.

                    MIRA (CONT'D)
     See? That's the smell of this exact moment. Right now. With
     you.

He takes the leaf, sniffs it. A private, thoughtful smile.

                    BEN
     I'll remember it.

He looks out at the park, thoughtful.

                    BEN (CONT'D)
     When I'm big, we'll live somewhere with a big tree. And you
     can sit in it all day and smell things.

Mira wraps an arm around him, pulls him close.

                    MIRA
     It's a deal.

END FLASHBACK

EXT. VICTORY PLAZA - DAY

BACK TO SCENE - The Leader's voice cuts through the memory.

                            THE LEADER
Progress is no longer a request. It is a command. Our
command. Your command.

He speaks of unity, sacrifice, purification. His voice is calm,
measured, chilling.

                       THE LEADER (CONT'D)
And to ensure this progress, we have the best people. There
are no better people than our people. The tremendous minds at
the Bureau of Counter Intelligence...the incredible patriots in
the Bureau of Belligerent Blunder Heads—though they want
me to stop calling them that!

Scattered, nervous LAUGHTER from the crowd.

Mira closes her eyes. The ghost of her son's smile fades, replaced by
the official report. *Runaway. Found drowned. Case closed.*

A man near the front FAINTS. Two SECURITY GUARDS
efficiently drag him away. The Leader doesn't pause.

Mira sees one of the guards clearly. His badge reads: #8647. His face
is impassive, professional.

                            THE LEADER
The future belongs to us. Seize it. Demand it. Become it. For
Change. For Progress. For the Republic!

The final ROAR is deafening. The Leader offers a sharp nod, turns,
and is gone.

The recorded fanfare BLARES. The crowd begins to disperse.

Mira remains still. The hollow dread has solidified into something
cold and permanent.

She kneels. The concrete is littered with debris and a fine gray ASH from iron braziers.

From her worn canvas bag, she pulls a small MASON JAR labeled "NOVEMBER."

She unscrews the lid. Uses it to sweep ash into the jar.

The heavy black BOOT of GUARD #8647 scuffs the concrete near her hand. He looks down at her, his gaze flat, assessing. He sees a woman gathering dirt. Harmless. He moves on.

Mira continues, methodical. She remembers the first jar, filled the night her son didn't come home.

She screws the lid back on. Wipes her gray fingers on her coat. Stands.

The plaza is nearly empty. Clean-up CREWS hose down the concrete.

Mira places the jar in her bag, next to the photograph. She turns her back on Victory Plaza and walks away.

INT. BUREAU OF BELLIGERENT BLUNDER HEADS – NIGHT

A long, windowless conference room. Walls lined with maps, surveillance photos, reels of confiscated film. A table stretches the length of the room. At its head sits THE LEADER, calm and rigid. Around the table: senior CONFIDANTES in gray suits. Each has a notebook. Each waits for the Leader to speak.

THE LEADER

Rumors.
(beat)
They call themselves The Undercurrent. They leave marks on stone, whispers in the alleys.

One confidante clears his throat nervously.

CONFIDANTE #1

We've traced symbols to four districts. A drainpipe, a market wall, even near the Cathedral itself. Small things. Perhaps just vandalism.

Another confidante—bold, careless—leans forward.

CONFIDANTE #2

Polard, if these are—

The Leader's hand SLAMS the table. A sharp crack. Silence.

THE LEADER

Never call me that again.

(icy)

Polard Mundt is dead. I am the Leader. Do you understand?

The confidante lowers his head, stammering apologies. The others avert their eyes.

The Leader composes himself, voice even, precise.

THE LEADER (CONT'D)

These marks are not small. They are seeds. Left unchecked, they grow. We do not permit growth outside our will.

He raises a finger. A door opens. SEVEN AGENTS enter, dressed in darker gray than the rest. Their faces are scarred, disciplined, anonymous.

THE LEADER (CONT'D)

You are the Task Force. You will hunt The Undercurrent. You will interrogate. You will cleanse. At any cost.

The agents stand at attention. The confidantes nod obediently, though unease ripples through them.

The Leader smiles thinly.

> THE LEADER (CONT'D)
> Progress does not whisper. Progress silences.

FADE BACK TO:

EXT. CITY STREETS - LATER

Mira walks through decaying streets. She passes the new HALL OF HISTORICAL CORRECTIONS.

She avoids the CATHEDRAL OF SILENCE, its immense doors shut tight. A place of terrifying rumor.

SOUND of a faint, complex SAXOPHONE RIFF from a basement: THE JAZZ CLUB.

EXT. MARKET SQUARE - CONTINUOUS

Mira cuts through a semi-official market. Stalls sell pathetic-looking vegetables and state-approved gray loaves.

At one stall, a man sells small, hand-carved wooden birds. Mira's step hitches. Ben loved birds.

She approaches. The birds are crude but full of life.

> VENDOR
> (Fluid, quiet)
> A finch for your windowsill? Keeps the silence away.

Mira reaches out to touch a small sparrow.

A WHISTLE BLARES. Two PUBLIC MORALITY OFFICERS shove through the crowd.

                              OFFICER
             Unauthorized commerce! This stall is closed!

The VENDOR doesn't argue. He sweeps the birds into a sack. He
catches Mira's eye and gives a tiny, imperceptible shake of his head.
Don't.

He melts into the crowd. The Officers kick over his empty stall.

Mira moves on, the encounter a fresh pinprick of fear.

EXT. CITY STREET – NIGHT

The sky glows faint orange with refinery smoke. Mira passes the
looming CATHEDRAL OF SILENCE. Its great iron doors are sealed,
but faint vibrations roll through the street—like a heartbeat muffled
by stone. She pauses, unsettled.

A loudspeaker crackles overhead.

                            VOICE (O.S.)
           Curfew begins in fifteen minutes. All citizens return home.
           Progress demands obedience.

As she walks faster, a sudden SHRIEK cuts the air—a man dragged
from an alley by GUARDS. His mouth moves, but no sound comes
out. They force him toward the Cathedral doors. He pounds at the air
with invisible words. Mira freezes, horrified.

The doors open a slit. A pale light leaks out, along with a silence
deeper than death. The man is shoved inside. The doors slam shut.
The vibrations cease.

Mira waits, breath held. She expects the city's noise to resume—
distant traffic, shouts, the hum of the grid. Nothing. For a few
seconds, the world is muted, as if the Cathedral's silence has spread

beyond its walls. Then sound trickles back, faint and thinned. She walks faster, unnerved by the thought that silence is not contained, but contagious.

Mira clutches her bag tighter, hurrying away, her pulse pounding with the echo of what she's seen.

She passes the public library. A new sign: "THE LIBRARY OF ERRORS." Windows dark. Closed for "review."

She looks past the dark library to the skyline. The TOWER OF SONG glows faintly, its music straining to break free. For one second, the haunting ARIA slips through the static, piercing her ears.

Then: SIRENS. A black drone swoops overhead, emitting a piercing counter-frequency that snuffs the melody. Sparks rain from the Tower's upper balconies. She sees shadows of musicians in chains being marched back inside.

One of the musicians breaks free, rushing toward the balcony rail. His mouth opens in a desperate cry, but no sound emerges. Guards drag him back inside. The Tower flickers once and dims. Mira realizes the silence doesn't just imprison—it unthreads voices completely.

The music dies, replaced by silence. Mira's dread hardens.

She finally reaches her apartment building.

INT. MIRA'S APARTMENT – LATER

A small, cramped space. Silent.

On a shelf: ELEVEN MASON JARS. Each labeled with a month, JANUARY-OCTOBER.

Mira places the new jar at the end. NOVEMBER.

She sets the photograph of Ben on the shelf in front of the jars.

She stands there, looking at them, as the light fades.

The SOUND of a door slamming downstairs. Fast, urgent FOOTSTEPS on the stairs.

The apartment door flies open.

Her sister, LENA (40's), stands there, pale, breathing hard. In her outstretched hand is a small, gray piece of paper. A receipt.

                              LENA
                      (voice raw, torn)
              He's gone. They took him. Last night.

INT. MIRA'S APARTMENT - LATER

Lena trembles, clutching the receipt.

                              LENA
              Men came. After curfew. They had papers. Official. Stamped.
              They said...questioning. About his work at the power station.

Mira takes the paper. Reads: "Detainee: Tomasz Varga. Reason: Administrative Review..."

                              LENA
              This is all they left.

Mira hands it back. Her voice is flat.

                              MIRA
              You go to the Precinct Office on Sovereign Avenue. You
              stand in line. It will be long. You wait. You show them this.
              They will tell you the review is ongoing. They will tell you to
              go home. To wait.

                              LENA

     Wait for what?

                              MIRA

     They will not say. You will go back the next day. You will do
     this until you stop going.

The terrible futility settles over them. Lena sinks onto a chair.

Mira turns away, steps out onto the small balcony.

EXT. BALCONY - CONTINUOUS

Cold air hits her face. A few scraggly plants. One small ROSE BUSH,
with two last, dying blooms.

Mira reaches out, traces a cool, velvety petal.

A sharp, black THORN snags her thumb. A single, perfect bead of
BLOOD wells up.

From inside, the muffled sound of Lena's sobs.

Mira steps back inside, walks to the shelf, and picks up the November
jar. She presses her bleeding thumb against the cool glass, right over
the label.

She smears it. A single, dark red streak across "NOVEMBER."

The glass door slides open. Lena stands there, eyes red. She sees
Mira's hand, the blood, the smear on the jar.

Their eyes lock. No words.

Lena's lips press into a thin, hard line. She gives a single, tiny nod.

She turns back into the apartment.

LENA

I need tea. Strong tea.

Mira places the jar back on the shelf. The red streak faces the room.

INT. DAILY BEACON PRESSROOM - DAY

The air tastes of ink, dust, and defeat. ELIAS (50's, weary) stands at his desk.

He reads the morning briefing sheet: *"LEADER HAILS RECORD HARVEST IN SECTOR 7."*

He knows it's a lie from the Hall of Historical Corrections. His cousin's last letter spoke of blight and ration cuts.

He taps out the required lies, polishing them. He saves the piece, sends it without a byline.

His real work waits in the basement.

INT. NEWSPAPER ARCHIVES/BASEMENT - LATER

A vast, cold room. Metal shelves stretch into shadows.

A YOUNG MAN in gray overalls mumbles about *"Batch Seven,"* pointing to a pallet of stained cardboard boxes.

Elias unlocks the heavy FURNACE ROOM door. A blast of heat. The dull ROAR of the fire.

He drags a box inside, cuts the twine. Pulls out a bound volume of the Beacon from five years prior. Headlines about real protests, genuine investigations.

He tosses the entire volume into the flames. He watches the pages blacken, curl, vanish.

He works, feeding the furnace, feeding the great silence.

He reaches into a box of loose papers, scoops up a handful, tosses them. One small, charred SCRAP lands near his boot.

He bends, picks it up. It's hot against his fingers. A fragment of text: "...*WAS LIAR AND THIEF. EVIDENCE...*"

He doesn't think. He folds the scrap tight, pushes it deep into his trouser pocket.

He slams the furnace door shut.

INT. DAILY BEACON PRESSROOM - LATER

Back at his desk, Elias' terminal glows with a new assignment: "*Commemorate One Year of Progress Initiative.*"

He lets his fingers hover over the keys, cold and stiff.

His gaze drifts to a bottom drawer. He pulls it open. A small stack of letters from his daughter, JENNA. He hasn't opened the last three.

He picks up the most recent. Her neat, angry writing fills the page. Accusations he deserves. She mentions a propaganda film he wrote the narration for. *She said her mother would not recognize the man he had become.*

He puts it down. He looks at the terminal. The cursor blinks.

He places his hands on the keys and begins to type the hollow, glittering lies. He saves the draft, sends it.

He opens the drawer again, looks at the unopened letters. He pulls out a blank sheet, picks up a pen. Hovers. No words come that aren't lies. He puts the pen down.

The scrap in his pocket feels heavier.

The shift bell CLANGS. Elias stands, gathers nothing, and walks out.

EXT. RIVERBANK - LATER

Elias stands on the bank, looking at the dark, slow-moving water.

He pulls out the folded scrap, unfolds it. The words clear: "...*WAS LIAR*..."

A gust of wind SNATCHES the paper. It flutters, lands on the greasy water, floats for a second, then darkens and sinks. Vanishes. Gone.

He stares at the spot. Empty-handed. He turns away.

INT. ELIAS' APARTMENT - NIGHT

The apartment is silent, lonely. A single photo on the mantel: a younger Elias, a smiling woman (his wife, ALMA), and a young JENNA.

Elias doesn't look at it. He goes to the kitchen, opens a nearly empty cupboard. He takes out a bottle of cheap liquor and a single, chipped glass.

He pours a glass and drinks it in one go. The burn is a feeling, at least.

He pours another. His hand shakes.

EXT. SOVEREIGN AVENUE/PRECINCT OFFICE - DAY

A long, slow-moving line of hollow-eyed, fearful people. Mira stands with Lena.

A WOMAN in front of them turns slightly, doesn't look at them, whispers.

                              WOMAN
They took my boy last week. They'll say anything...But...
look for the marks. On the walls. On the pavement. Near the
drains. They point the way.

                               MIRA
What marks?

                              WOMAN
The quiet ones.

The woman turns away.

Finally, it's Lena's turn. A bored CLERK takes the receipt, types the
number.

                              CLERK
Review is ongoing. Next.

                               LENA
But where is he? Can I bring him anything?

                              CLERK
                      (eyes devoid of empathy)
Next.

Mira leads her numb sister away.

EXT. CITY STREET - LATER

On the walk back, Mira's eyes scan the walls, the pavement. Then she
sees it. Faint, scratched into the paint on a drainpipe: a small, simple
symbol. A wave.

She stops, pulls Lena to a halt, points.

They look at it. A message. A sign. They are not alone.

The Undercurrent is real.

INT. ELIAS' APARTMENT - NIGHT

Elias sits in a worn armchair. The light is low. He holds a small, plain NOTEBOOK. His daughter's.

He opens it. Only a single line in his daughter's neat, precise handwriting on the first page. All other pages are blank.

He reads it. Closes the cover. Places it on the table.

He goes to the cupboard, takes out the bottle. Pours a glass, drinks it down. Then another and another.

The words from the notebook remain perfectly clear.

THE TRUTH IS A WIDOW WHO OUTLIVES HER EULOGIES.

He looks at the notebook. It feels heavy as lead.

EXT. CATHEDRAL OF PROGRESS - DAY

A stark, imposing structure of steel and glass. A single needle-like spire. A massive stained-glass window high above: a single, unblinking HUMAN EYE.

A great CROWD stands in the square, perfectly silent.

Mira is among them. Elias stands near the press reporters, official notebook in hand, hungover.

THE LEADER stands on a high platform. A CHOIR OF BOYS in white robes sings a hymn.

Mira watches the boys. One, near the back, sings a half-beat behind, his eyes scanning the crowd with fear.

As the song ends, the boy brings his hands together in a clap. His cuff pulls back. Mira sees letters stitched inside with red thread: "*REMEMBER*." The cuff falls back.

The Leader speaks, his voice a hypnotic drone.

The SOUND of the TOWER OF SONG's mournful melody weaves through the gaps in his speech, a haunting counterpoint. The Leader's eye twitches, almost imperceptibly. He cannot silence it.

An OLD WOMAN leans toward Mira, whispers.

                              OLD WOMAN
          They came for my neighbor. For singing old songs. I told the
          rent collector. They gave me a can of meat. The sugar was
          very sweet.

The woman disappears into the crowd.

Elias writes down the Leader's hollow words. He looks past him, sees a WORKMAN on scaffolding, slumped with exhaustion. Their eyes meet across the square.

A moment of perfect, silent understanding. Then the worker looks down.

The Leader finishes. A raised hand. Blessing and dismissal.

The crowd begins to disperse.

High above, the choir files down. The boy with the red thread catches his sleeve on sharp metal. A single long red thread UNRAVELS, catches the wind.

It lifts into the air, a thin red line against the gray sky. It catches for a moment on the tip of the golden spire, then pulls free, carried away over the rooftops.

Mira watches it until it vanishes.

Her eyes drop. There, on the pristine new curbstone, is a fresh mark. Etched into the stone: the wave symbol of The Undercurrent.

Her heart quickens. *They were here.*

Elias walks away as if in a trance. He knows the article he must write will be a masterpiece of obfuscation. A betrayal.

EXT. BACK ALLEY NEAR MARKET – NIGHT

Mira keeps her hood low, clutching the jar in her bag. From a side street, she sees the Task Force raid the market.

Agents smash stalls, tear cloth from awnings, spill grain across the cobblestones. Merchants beg as their goods are destroyed. A mother clutches her child, screaming.

AGENT KEISTER steps forward, cold and deliberate.

> KEISTER
> Voices do not belong to you. Voices belong to the Leader.

He signals. An agent wrenches the child away. The mother collapses, muffled by a black cloth forced over her mouth.

Mira presses herself flat against the wall, barely breathing. She grips the photograph so hard it bends in her fist.

> KEISTER (CONT'D)
> (to the crowd)
> When you whisper, you drown. When you drown, no one saves you.

Silence. Only the sound of boots as the Task Force marches off, dragging captives.

Mira exhales shakily, stepping out from the shadows.

> MIRA
> (whispering to herself)
> They're hunting us now.

She disappears into the dark.

EXT. ALLEYWAY - LATER

Mira doesn't go home. She follows a route she now realizes she's been unconsciously mapping for months. She turns into a narrow, grimy alley.

She finds it. Another wave, freshly scrawled in chalk on a brick wall. And beneath it, another symbol: a small, crudely drawn sparrow.

Her breath catches. She remembers the market, the wooden bird, Ben in the tree. A sign within a sign. For her?

She hears a SCRAPE behind her. She turns, heart hammering. But the alley is empty. A shadow detaches itself from a doorway further down and slips away around a corner.

She is not alone. She is being seen.

Mira turns to leave. The Cathedral stands, a permanent claim on the skyline.

But she holds onto the images he did not intend: the boy's fear, the red thread, the worker's exhaustion, the tiny etched wave, the sparrow.

The Cathedral was meant to be the end of the story.

For Mira, for Elias, for the unknown hand that etched the symbol, it is the beginning.

FADE OUT.

END OF PART ONE

Part II

EXT. BUTTON FACTORY - NIGHT

A derelict building. A single string of BARE ELECTRIC BULBS hangs from the low ceiling.

People sit crowded on crates. All faces are turned toward ROSA (40's, fierce intelligence), who stands before a small wooden table with TWELVE WATER GLASSES, each filled to a different level.

She runs her wet finger around the rim of the first glass. A single, pure, resonant NOTE blooms. She plays a pattern. Short and long tones. The same sequence three times.

Some in the audience have their eyes closed, translating the notes into letters. The letters form a word: *REMEMBER*.

The last note fades.

Then—

CRASH!

The heavy wooden door EXPLODES inward. Bright white light floods in, silhouetting several tall figures in GRAY UNIFORMS.

They move down the stairs with brutal efficiency. The crowd rises—a sharp, collective INTAKE of breath.

A GUARD walks to Rosa's table. Picks up a glass. Examines it. Opens his hand. The glass SMASHES on the concrete. He picks up another. Drops it. SMASH. Another. SMASH. Methodically destroying all twelve.

Another guard finds a trumpet case. STOMPS on it. Finds a clarinet. SNAPS it over his knee.

They are erasing all sound.

The guards motion for the people to leave. The crowd files out, silent.

Rosa remains, hands at her sides, staring at the shards.

The guard who broke the glasses points to the door. She doesn't move. He takes a step closer, raises his hand to push her.

A low, steady HUMMING starts at the back of the room. A MAN with his eyes closed, humming the first note of the sequence—'R'.

A WOMAN joins him. Then another. The hum grows, a deep, resonant frequency that fills the basement.

A sound from their bodies. A sound that cannot be broken.

The guard stops, confused. He lowers his hand. He looks at Rosa one last time, then turns and leaves with the others.

The hum continues. The people carry it with them as they scatter into the night.

The guard's badge is visible: #8647.

INT. UNDERGROUND SHELTER – NIGHT

Rosa unrolls old sheet music. Ink smudged, edges frayed. Mira leans close.

MIRA
<blockquote>It's dangerous to keep this.</blockquote>

ROSA
<blockquote>It's dangerous to forget.</blockquote>

She runs her fingers over the notes.

136

ROSA (CONT'D)

They say the Cathedral doesn't only erase sound. It hoards it. Every cry, every song—it's all trapped inside.

Rosa presses her palms to her ears, but the silence she's heard lingers inside, gnawing. For a moment she fears her own voice is gone. She whispers her name to test. The sound comes faint, thinner than before. She shudders, wondering if every brush with the Cathedral takes something permanent.

EXT. CITY STREETS - NIGHT

Rosa walks. From a nearby alley, the hum—a low, sustained note from a man in shadows. A woman passing echoes it, then turns a corner.

The hum is alive. Spreading.

EXT. CATHEDRAL OF SILENCE – NIGHT

Rosa walks past the Cathedral. Tonight, the doors are slightly open. She hears muffled gasps inside—hundreds of voices straining against the silence. A GUARD slams them shut, but not before a single NOTE escapes, piercing the night like a blade.

Rosa stops breathing. The NOTE lingers in her bones. She realizes: the Cathedral doesn't only erase sound. It hoards it.

A GUARD notices her staring. She walks away fast, her heart hammering.

INT. ROSA'S APARTMENT - NIGHT

Rosa enters her small, sparse apartment. She leans against the closed door, breathing heavily.

She walks to the sink, pours a glass of water. Her hands are still shaking. She looks at the glass, sees the ghost of the one the guard smashed.

Anger flashes in her eyes. She raises the glass as if to throw it. Stops herself. Instead, she drinks, the water a cold, defiant act of preservation.

INT. MIRA'S APARTMENT BUILDING LOBBY - DAY

Mira listens as a woman at the water queue turns, murmurs.

> WOMAN
> They broke the music last night. Near the old factory. But they couldn't break the tune.

Mira's eyes meet the woman's. A new, hard light is in them. Mira feels a jolt of fear, then a surge of fierce pride.

INT. MIRA'S APARTMENT - LATER

Mira is at her shelf of ash jars. She picks up the NOVEMBER jar, the one with her blood smeared on it. She holds it tightly.

She opens the lid. The faint, acrid scent of the ash fills her nostrils. It is the smell of the plaza, of the Leader's words.

She closes her eyes, not to remember the rally, but to remember the park from her flashback. The smell of honeysuckle and cut grass. She holds the jar of ash in one hand and the memory of the leaf in the other.

The memory is more potent. She screws the lid back on, her resolve hardening. She will not let them erase the good smells.

INT. DAILY BEACON PRESSROOM - DAY

ELIAS reads a tersely worded memo. He types, fingers numb.

INSERT - MEMO: "A seditionist meeting hall used for anti-progress ideological trafficking was shut down by vigilant authorities."

He knows it came from the Bureau of Belligerent Blunder Heads. He types the lies. Each word a betrayal of the hum he now carries.

INT. DAILY BEACON PRESSROOM - LATER

Elias' terminal pings. A new, priority memo. It's a list of approved synonyms. The phrase "shut down" is to be replaced with "cleansed." "Authorities" is to be replaced with "Guardians."

He highlights his just-finished article and mechanically replaces the words. The text becomes even more sterile and sinister. "The hall was cleansed by the Guardians."

He feels a profound nausea. He is not just reporting on the cleaning; he is performing it with language.

EXT. CITY - MONTAGE

    — A FATHER hums the sequence as a lullaby to his young child.
    — WORKERS hum it softly as they repair a road.
    — The symbol of the WAVE appears—scratched on a bench, chalked on a wall.
    — The hum is the heartbeat of the resistance. Quiet. Steady.

END MONTAGE

INT. ROSA'S SAFEHOUSE – NIGHT

Rosa tends to a half-dozen children, teaching them the forbidden notes. They hum softly, barely above a whisper. The sound trembles in the room like fragile glass.

ROSA

Softer. The world is listening.

The humming grows steady, fragile.

A sudden, pounding at the door.

CHILD
(whispering)

It's them.

Rosa's face hardens. She ushers the children toward a trapdoor. They crawl beneath the floorboards, covering themselves with scraps of burlap.

The pounding grows louder.

KEISTER (O.S.)

Open. Search order.

Rosa grabs a cloth and smears chalk across the sparrow and wave symbols on her wall, blurring it into nothing. She unlocks the door just as it bursts open.

The Task Force storms in. Agents scatter through the room, overturning chairs, smashing jars, ripping open cupboards. One kicks a pile of books into the fire. Pages curl and blacken.

Keister steps inside, calm amid the destruction. He circles Rosa.

KEISTER
Strange silence in this place. Too clean. Too careful.

ROSA

It is a home. Not a battlefield.

Keister studies her. Then, suddenly, he leans close, whispering in her ear.

KEISTER
(whispering)
The Undercurrent thinks it can hide in gutters. But all water runs into the Cathedral. Do you understand?

Rosa does not flinch.

                                  ROSA
          I understand fear. And I know yours is greater.

A flicker of anger crosses KEISTER's face, but he pulls back. He
signals the squad.

                                KEISTER
          Leave her. For now.

The Task Force files out, leaving the room in ruins. Rosa stands
shaking. She kneels, pulls back the trapdoor.

The children crawl out, their faces pale with terror. One clings to her
skirt.
                                 CHILD
                              (whispering)
          Why didn't they take us?

Rosa holds him close, eyes burning.

                                  ROSA
          Because we will not be taken. Not yet.

EXT. CITY STREET – DAY

The Undercurrent Task Force moves in formation, gray uniforms
darker than the Guards. Their leader, AGENT KEISTER, surveys a
street market. His eyes are cold, precise.

He signals. Agents smash stalls with batons, upend baskets, scatter
food. They spray black paint over scratched wave symbols.

A YOUNG MAN is dragged from the crowd. He's shoved against a
wall.

                                KEISTER
          Do you hum? Do you carry their song?

The man shakes his head desperately. Keister nods. An agent jams a steel funnel into the man's mouth. They pour thick gray paste down his throat—state rations hardened into silence. He gags, collapses. The crowd watches, frozen. No one dares move.

Keister signals the squad onward. Boots march in rhythm. Leaving destruction in their wake.

INT. TASK FORCE HOLDING ROOM – NIGHT

Fluorescent lights buzz overhead. A row of chairs, each occupied by BLINDFOLDED PRISONERS. Their hands bound. Their mouths gagged.

Agents move down the line, ripping away gags, barking questions.

> AGENT
> Say the sequence. Who taught you the notes?

The prisoners remain silent. One prisoner hums a faint tone—defiance. An agent smashes him across the face with a baton. Silence again.

Keister watches without expression. He marks a list on his clipboard, one word beside each prisoner: *KEEP* or *DISAPPEAR*.

EXT. SUBWAY TUNNEL – NIGHT

The Undercurrent gathers in the dark. Rosa leads Mira and a dozen others. They chalk the wave symbol on the tunnel wall, then light a lantern shielded with red cloth.

Suddenly, the tunnel quakes. A TRAIN SCREAMS past—unmarked, windowless. Inside, through the slits, Mira glimpses PRISONERS strapped to upright frames, mouths covered by black steel masks. Their eyes plead.

The train vanishes into the dark. The group stands frozen. Rosa whispers.

Her whisper barely carries. Mira frowns, realizing it wasn't just Rosa speaking softly—the tunnel itself swallowed half the sound. The silence is spreading, seeping like gas into the city's veins.

> ROSA
> (whispering)
> The Cathedral feeds on them.

They extinguish the lantern. The silence is unbearable.

INT. ROSA'S APARTMENT - DAY

Heavy silence. Rosa's mother AGATA (70's, serene strength) stands by the window, holding an old winter coat. Her fingers trace the worn fabric.

> AGATA
> The seam ripper. Please.

Rosa fetches the small metal tool. Her mother turns the coat inside out. With precise movements, she picks apart the stitches holding the lining.

She reaches into the opening. Pulls out a dense weave of many-colored threads—a tiny, intricate tapestry.

> AGATA
> It is a song. Banned. The colors are the notes. The weave holds the rhythm. The last movement of the Fourth Symphony.

Rosa stares, horror and dawning admiration. Her mother gestures to the other coats by the door.

AGATA (CONT'D)

All of them. An archive. They took the music from the air...so
I put it in the one thing everyone needs.

The brilliant insanity of it takes Rosa's breath away. Her mother
begins sewing the lining back up.

EXT. ROSA'S APARTMENT BUILDING - DAY

PEOPLE walk by the building, each one lost within their own world.
A silent march of progress, grudging through the bustling city streets.
No one even acknowledges the buildings existence. People pass each
other as they walk without so much as a nod passing between them.

EXT. ROSA'S APARTMENT - DAY

Two days later. A polite, quiet KNOCK on the door. Rosa opens it.
Two men in clean gray uniforms stand there, faces blank.

GUARD

Agata?

Rosa's mother steps forward.

AGATA

I am here.

She puts on her shoes, doesn't take a coat, and walks out between
them. Rosa stands in the doorway, alone.

INT. ROSA'S APARTMENT - NIGHT

Rosa does not cry. She moves with a furious, quiet purpose. She pulls
every coat from her mother's closet.

One by one, she turns them inside out, unpicks the linings, and
extracts the woven musical scores. She lays them out on the floor—a
symphony in textile.

She gets a needle and thread. She selects one score. She doesn't resew
it into a coat. Instead, she begins sewing it onto the inside of her own
jacket, over her heart. She will wear the music. She will be the
archive.

EXT. ROOFTOPS – NIGHT

Rosa climbs to a high roof, wearing the sewn tapestry beneath her
jacket. From here, the TOWER OF SONG is visible, chained in
scaffolding, ringed by guards. She presses her palm against her chest.
The woven notes hum faintly against her heart.

Suddenly, SPOTLIGHTS sweep the sky. A drone circles closer. Rosa
ducks behind a chimney. The drone emits a low-frequency pulse—her
jacket vibrates violently, trying to sing. She clamps a hand over her
chest, teeth clenched against the resonance.

For a terrible second, she thinks the song in her jacket will rip out of
her body, leaving her hollow. The thought chills her: silence doesn't
destroy. It consumes, leaving shells behind.

The drone passes. She gasps, sweat pouring down. The city is no
longer safe.

INT. INTERROGATION ROOM - DAY

A white room with a table and two chairs. A bright light overhead
hurts Elias' eyes.

Two GUARDS fire questions at him about his private thoughts, his
family and his daughter.

He tries to be clever, vague. Their questions are needles. He breaks
and words spill out. He confesses to the scrap of paper, the walk by
the river and the humming. He gives names—some real, some
invented.

When he is empty, they lead him out, put him on the street. He walks
home under a sun too bright. Hollowed out.

INT. ELIAS' APARTMENT - NIGHT

Elias scrubs his hands in the sink, raw and red. He can't get the feeling of the interrogation room off his skin.

He looks at the photo of his wife and daughter. His wife's face seems to turn away from him. He opens the drawer where he keeps his daughter's unread letters.

This time, he takes them all out. He doesn't read them. He simply holds them, a weight of disappointment and love. He knows he has betrayed the man they thought he was.

EXT. CITY - MONTAGE

— The hum migrates.
— In an ELEVATOR, a man hums a note. A woman picks it up.
— On a crowded TROLLEY, a harmonica plays three notes. The player pockets it.
— A CHILD hums.
— Rosa takes a NAIL and a HAMMER. In a quiet square, she stamps out the entire word in Morse code: REMEMBER.
— She etches it into a metal RAILING. Carves it into a wooden BENCH.
— A map of sound written on the city's skin.
— GUARD #8647 watches her from across the square, makes a note in a small book.

END MONTAGE

INT. HALL OF HISTORICAL CORRECTION - DAY

A vast, silent space. Sterile light falls on glass display cases. Each contains an ordinary object with a card explaining its "moral failure."

MIRA pushes a cleaning cart.

A CURATOR in a gray tunic approaches with a cardboard box.

CURATOR

New acquisitions. From the latest clarifications. Catalog them.

He hands her the box. She carries it to a back room, opens it. Inside: personal effects of the disappeared. A pocket watch. Spectacles. A wedding band. A small notebook.

Near the bottom, her fingers touch cold metal. She pulls out a PRESS BADGE. She recognizes the name engraved on it. The journalist.

FADE OUT.

END OF PART TWO

Part III

EXT. RIVERBANK - DAY

The brown water moves slowly. A solitary MAN (60's, dusty clothes, old pack) walks along the muddy bank.

He stops, kneels and digs with his bare fingers. He pulls free a strange object—a PRESS BADGE and a KEY, fused together by fine, dry PLANT ROOTS.

He washes it in the river, examines it and carries it to a clear spot. He gathers dry grass and twigs. He places the fused object on top.

He Strikes a match and lights the grass and twigs. Flames CRACKLE.

The roots and metal heat. Thick, white SMOKE rises. It forms shapes, letters, words—a NAME and a PHRASE—before the wind takes them.

The man watches, nods once, and continues his journey.

Further down the bank, MIRA watches. She recognizes the name in the smoke. Elias.

She looks at the circle of ash. A physical fact. She turns and walks back toward the city.

EXT. RIVERBEND - CONTINUOUS

Mira doesn't follow the path. She walks to the water's edge.

She kneels. With her finger, she draws in the wet sand: the wave symbol of the Undercurrent.

She watches as the river's gentle lap slowly erases it, grain by grain. The fight isn't for permanence, but for the constant act of redrawing the truth.

EXT. ABANDONED BOTANICAL GARDENS - DAY

Nature has run wild. ROSA walks, seeking silence.

She stops at a tree. Long, dry SEEDPODS hang like brown teardrops. She reaches up, takes one.

Its surface is rough, covered in small bumps arranged in deliberate patterns. Dots. She traces them. They spell a word. REMEMBER.

A GIRL (12, patched clothes, basket of foraged roots) steps from behind another tree.

                         GIRL
        My grandfather made these. He was a printer. Before they
        took him. He carved the words. The trees made them part of
        their seeds.

The girl reaches into her basket, pulls out a longer, more complex pod.

                           GIRL (CONT'D)
          This one has a message I haven't figured out yet.

She holds it out. Rosa takes it. The pod is heavy, meaningful.

The girl nods and disappears back into the green shadows.

Rosa closes her fingers around the pod. Truth that can be planted and grown.

EXT. CATHEDRAL OF SILENCE – DAY

A crowd gathers at the base of the Cathedral. The Leader himself arrives with guards. The massive doors open for the first time in daylight. Inside: endless rows of glass cylinders filled with vibrating fragments of sound—captured voices, stolen songs, choked screams. The Leader spreads his arms.

                           THE LEADER
          Here is the grave of chaos. Here, the silence that built our
          strength.

The crowd applauds nervously. But Mira, watching from the back, notices cracks spreading through the glass walls. The stolen sounds PRESS against their prisons. For a moment, she hears Ben's laughter echo—sharp, real, impossible.

She staggers back, overwhelmed.

INT. BUREAU OF BELLIGERENT BLUNDER HEADS – NIGHT

The Leader sits alone with Keister and three confidantes. The table is bare except for files. Photographs of the wave symbol. Sketches of sparrows. Confiscated scraps of paper with the word *"REMEMBER."*

THE LEADER
They still breathe. They still mark. And yet you tell me the
Task Force has cleansed?

Keister lowers his eyes.

KEISTER
They are slippery, Leader. They move through whispers and
scratches.

A confidante murmurs, too softly:

CONFIDANTE
(murmuring, softly)
Perhaps Polard—

The Leader turns, fury boiling.

THE LEADER
(furious)
Polard Mundt is dead. Dead! You will bury that name, or I
will bury you.

The confidante trembles. He nods.

The Leader leans forward, almost whispering.

THE LEADER (CONT'D)
The Cathedral swells with their stolen voices. But it is not
enough. I want them all. No one escapes.

Keister straightens.

KEISTER
We will break the Undercurrent, Leader. Every mark, every
note, erased.

The Leader allows a small, cold smile.

THE LEADER
Good. Because if you fail me again, you will be erased first.

INT. ROSA'S APARTMENT - NIGHT

Rosa sits at her small table. The complex seedpod is in front of her. Next to it, a sheet of paper and a pencil.

She runs her fingertips over the bumps, again and again. She is trying to feel its meaning.

She closes her eyes. Her fingers trace the patterns. She remembers the feel of the water glasses. The vibration of the hum.

Her hand picks up the pencil and draws: not letters, but a single, continuous line that loops and knots itself into a complex, beautiful symbol. It is a word, a map, a melody, and a seed.

She opens her eyes and looks at what she has drawn. She understands. The word isn't meant to be read. It's meant to be felt.

EXT. GRANITE QUARRY - DAY

A vast, gaping wound in the earth.

A great gray cloud of PIGEONS rises from the city, flies straight east, and settles on the high ledges of the quarry walls by the thousands.

Their soft COOING begins. It echoes off the stone walls, amplifies, deepens into a rolling, resonant DRONE. A single, resonant HUM. A natural AMEN.

The sound vibrates through the stone, through the earth.

INT. ROSA'S APARTMENT - CONTINUOUS

Rosa feels the vibration through the soles of her feet. She puts down the seedpod, leaves her building.

INT. MIRA'S APARTMENT - CONTINUOUS

Mira feels the hum in the air. She goes to her window, then out her door.

EXT. QUARRY RIM - CONTINUOUS

Rosa and Mira arrive separately, look down into the great bowl. The sound washes over them.

They see the pigeons covering the cliffs like a living extension of the rock.

This is the opposite of the Cathedral. An honest absence. A celebration of decay.

Mira climbs down the dusty path. Takes a small vial, collects some of the fine gray powder. Verdict residue.

MRS. NOVA arrives, stands on the rim. Her eyes find the rusted scrap-metal SAXOPHONE lying on a flat rock. A relic of human grief, now silent.

The sound continues. People begin to arrive. Alone, in pairs, in small groups. Some stand on the rim, some climb down. They listen. The sound asks nothing of them.

A single, nervous GUARD arrives. He stands on the rim, writes down "8647" on his report. He sees people standing silently, listening to birds. No signs. No chants. No leaders. He leaves, frustrated. His report: "Citizens observing local wildlife. No actionable dissent detected."

EXT. QUARRY FLOOR - LATER

As the sun lowers, the crowd thins. Rosa remains.

She sees a figure approaching through the settling dust. It's Mira. They look at each other, a silent acknowledgment—the musician and the archivist of ash.

They do not speak. They simply stand together for a moment, two points of stillness in the vast, humming bowl.

Then Mira turns and walks back up the path. Rosa stays a moment longer, then follows.

The sun sets. The stars emerge. The people slowly leave, carrying the hum back with them in their bodies.

EXT. VICTORY PLAZA - DAY

A vast, empty expanse of stone. Silent.

At its center, the BRONZE STATUE of the Leader, green with patina, thick with MOSS.

A BIOLOGY STUDENT (20's) stands at its base with a clipboard. She measures a hairline fracture running up the statue's calf.

BIOLOGY STUDENT
(muttering)
Structural integrity compromised. Moss roots exacerbating fractures. Eventual failure in fifteen to twenty years.

A dispassionate verdict from nature itself.

Mira watches from a stone bench. Her eyes move to the marble inscription. The original words *"FOR THE PEOPLE"* have been etched by acidic pigeon droppings. They now read: *"FOR THE PIGEONS."*

Mrs. Nova walks into the plaza. She sees the transformed statue, the altered inscription. She reads it. A sharp exhalation escapes her—not quite a laugh, a release.

Mira walks to the base, ignores the towering figure. She uses a spoon to scrape a sample of white marble dust mixed with green moss into a vial. Seals it. Labels it. Verdict residue.

The biology student packs up and leaves. Mrs. Nova shakes her head and walks away.

The statue stands, waiting. Its surface slowly being eaten.

EXT. VICTORY PLAZA - LATER

A light RAIN begins to fall.

Mira doesn't leave. She watches the rain trace paths through the grime on the statue's face.

A street sweeper appears. He doesn't sweep the plaza. Instead, he stops before the statue, looks up at the transformed inscription: *"FOR THE PIGEONS."*

He chuckles to himself, a low, raspy sound. Then he gets to work, not clearing the pigeon droppings, but carefully sweeping around them, preserving the new message.

EXT. LANDFILL - DAY

A vast landscape of waste.

Mira walks narrow paths. A flash of color: a PAPER POSTCARD, half-buried. A picture of a perfect beach. Something green is growing from its center—a small, determined SHOOT.

Mira bends, reads the faded writing on the back: a message of missing someone, a promise to be home soon. Signed with a child's name. Thrown away, but the paper held a seed.

EXT. LANDFILL SETTLEMENT - DAY

Huts made of scrap wood and metal sheeting. ANYA (10), finds a spent BULLET CASING. She wipes off the dirt.

Nearby, a wilted SEEDLING grows by a leaky pipe. Anya fills the casing with damp soil, carefully transplants the seedling into it. Presses the soil gently and puts it on her windowsill.

She waters it each day.

The plant grows stronger. The leaves turn deep green. It puts out a bud that opens into a FLOWER that glows with a soft VIOLET LIGHT.

At dusk, the flower produces a low, pure HUM.

Anya names it Tuesday.

INT. SETTLEMENT SCHOOL - DAY

A single room. A TIRED TEACHER instructs from old books. Anya shows her the flower.

> TIRED TEACHER
> It's a weed. No use. It bears no fruit. Cannot be eaten. A distraction.

Anya holds the plant in her lap, feels the gentle hum through her fingers. A truth that exists outside official categories.

The hum continues each dusk. A quiet, undeniable presence.

EXT. SUBWAY TUNNEL – NIGHT

Mira hurries through the tunnels. Behind her: the echo of boots. The Task Force is sweeping the underground, sealing exits, dragging prisoners into trucks.

She ducks into a side shaft, barely escaping a beam of flashlight. Agents pass close, one muttering:

AGENT
The Leader wants the girl alive.

Mira clamps a hand over her mouth, trembling. The photograph slips from her grasp, falling to the floor. She catches it just before it hits the water.

The Task Force continues deeper into the tunnels. Their voices fade, but the bootsteps remain.

Mira presses forward, crawling through the shaft until it opens into a forgotten junction. She stops, gasping. Her hands shake as she lifts the photograph. The image is smudged, almost erased.

She whispers to it, broken:

MIRA
(whispering)
I can't lose you too.

A low whistle echoes from far ahead—a signal. The Undercurrent is close.

Mira pushes herself up, forces her legs to move, and runs into the dark.

EXT. VICTORY PLAZA – NIGHT

The statue of the Leader looms. Guards patrol.

Suddenly, from the Tower of Song, a single defiant trumpet BLASTS into the night—raw, human, unstoppable. The sound rips through the plaza. The statue trembles. Pigeons explode into the air.

The guards panic. One SHOUTS into a radio. The Leader himself emerges from the Cathedral across the square, his face twisted. He raises his hand—signals the Cathedral doors.

They swing wide. The stolen silence floods out, a black wave of absence. It SLAMS against the trumpet's song. For a heartbeat, the world hangs between sound and nothing.

The trumpet BLASTS from the Tower of Song. The plaza shakes. The Leader emerges from the Cathedral, his smile tight.

The Cathedral doors open. The stolen silence surges out—a black, pulsing void. It collides with the trumpet's defiance.

For one unbearable instant, sound and silence tear at each other, shredding the air. Windows burst. People collapse, clutching their ears.

Then—quiet.

The trumpet is gone. The Tower stands dark, one final ember extinguished.

In the plaza, the crowd looks around, dazed. Lips move, but no words emerge. Mothers scream silently for their children. Guards shout unheard orders. The world has gone mute.

Mira clutches Rosa's arm. She tries to speak—nothing. Rosa opens her mouth. Nothing. The hum, the heartbeat of the Undercurrent, has been drowned.

The Leader steps forward. His voice cuts through the void, the only sound left.

THE LEADER

    At last. Unity.

His words echo across the square, unstoppable. He raises his arms. The crowd falls to its knees, not in reverence, but in terror.

Mira looks at Rosa. Their eyes lock. Tears stream silently down their faces. In Rosa's pocket, the seed pod trembles faintly.

BLACK SCREEN.

A single faint vibration carries under the silence. Not music. Not words. Only the ache of something once alive.

INT. CATHEDRAL OF SILENCE – NIGHT

The voices crash through the Cathedral. Agents fall, writhing, consumed by light. Keister reaches for Mira—then vanishes into the roar.

Silence slams down. Heavy. Absolute. Mira trembles, gripping the photograph.

The great doors CREAK.

The LEADER enters. Alone. His gray cloak drags against the stones. His face is unreadable, cold as carved stone.

He surveys the ruin of his Task Force. Bodies strewn. Torches extinguished. Dust in the air like smoke after battle.

                    THE LEADER
          So. The little sparrow sings.

Mira turns to face him. Her voice shakes but does not break.

                    MIRA
          You can't hold them anymore. They've broken through.

The Leader steps closer, boots echoing unnaturally loud in the silence.

                    THE LEADER
                 (soft, venomous)
          There is no "they." Only what I permit. Even these walls…
                    (gestures)
          …were raised by my will.

Mira clutches the photograph tighter.

MIRA

You've stolen too much. You've eaten too many voices. Even stone can't carry that weight.

The Leader studies her—almost pitying.

THE LEADER

You think this is rebellion? It's collapse. Without me, only chaos remains.

He extends his hand.

THE LEADER (CONT'D)
Give me the picture. Relinquish the ache. Be silent. Be free.

The Cathedral HUMS—low, ominous. The stones seem to reject his words. A hairline crack splits the altar.

Mira shakes her head.

MIRA
I won't give you what you can't destroy.

The hum swells. The stolen voices rise again, louder, pouring from the walls. The Leader stiffens, his composure cracking for the first time.

THE LEADER
(raising his voice)
I am silence! I am the end of noise!

But the Cathedral does not obey. The voices rise higher, crashing like a tidal wave. The arches tremble. Light bursts through fissures in the walls.

Mira staggers, blinded. She clutches the photograph to her chest.

The Leader screams—not words, but raw sound—as the Cathedral swallows him. His body twists in the white light, breaking apart into shards of shadow.

Then—absolute silence.

The Cathedral stands still. Empty. The torches are gone. The dust settles.

Mira opens her eyes. She is alone. The photograph glows faintly in her hands, edges burning soft with light, as if the voices now live inside it.

She collapses to her knees. Exhausted. Trembling. Alive.

FADE OUT.

EPILOGUE

INT. CATHEDRAL OF SILENCE – NIGHT

The Cathedral is still. Mira kneels at the altar, clutching the glowing photograph. Dust drifts down like snow.

She staggers to her feet and stumbles toward the great doors. They open without sound. She steps into the night.

EXT. VICTORY PLAZA – DAWN

The sky is pale gray. The massive screens that once projected the Leader's face flicker with static. No image. No voice. Just blank silence.

Crowds gather, uncertain, whispering. Some dare to hum—low, tentative notes that ripple through the plaza. The sound spreads. Small, fragile. Alive.

Guards watch from the edges, confused, leaderless. None move. None silence the people.

INT. ROSA'S SAFEHOUSE – MORNING

Rosa tends to the children. She presses a finger to her lips, urging quiet. But then she hears it: faint humming from outside, growing stronger.

She opens the shutters a crack. Neighbors in the street hum together, heads lifted. For the first time, no Guards break them apart.

A tear slips down Rosa's cheek.

EXT. CITY OUTSKIRTS – DAY

Mira walks alone down a dirt road, exhausted, barefoot, the photograph clutched to her chest. The glow has faded, leaving only the smudged, almost-erased image.

She pauses. A sparrow lands on the road ahead of her, tilts its head, then takes flight. Mira follows, her steps slow but steady.

INT. BUREAU OF BELLIGERENT BLUNDER HEADS – DAY

The long table. Empty chairs. Papers scattered. The Leader's seat is vacant.

Confidantes whisper nervously among themselves.

                    CONFIDANTE #1
                      (whispering)
          Without him, what remains?

                    CONFIDANTE #2
          Order. Discipline. Or ruin.

Silence. No one sits in the Leader's chair.

EXT. VICTORY PLAZA – NIGHT

Thousands gather, filling the square. Candles flicker in their hands. The humming swells into song—uneven, untrained, but unstoppable.

Above them, the giant screens still flicker, blank. For the first time in years, nothing fills the sky. Only their voices.

EXT. HILL OUTSIDE CITY – NIGHT

Mira stands alone, overlooking the city. She hears the faint rise of song from the plaza below.

She presses the photograph to her heart.

> MIRA
> (whispering)
> You're still here.

The wind carries the sound of the voices to her. The city glows faintly, no longer silent.

Mira's face is tired, lined with grief, but she allows herself the smallest, broken smile.

FADE OUT.

THE HOLY ACHE OF THE UNBECOMING

About the Author

Laughton J. Collins, Jr. was born in the 20th century but currently lives in the 21st century. He is originally from Georgia—currently living somewhere in the Pacific Northwest—in and/or around the Seattle area— His work has been published in resurrection magazine issue II: crucify, March 31, 2024.

Also by Laughton J. Collins, Jr.

1. ghost riders in the sky and other lines (2023)
2. J^M!3– Anthology: Volume I (2024)
3. Shadows & Light: Haiku/Senryū (2024)
4. ghost riders in the sky and other lines (deluxe edition) (2024)
5. Paper View (2025)
6. The God Who Breaks: Old Testament Plays of Rebellion and Despair (2025)
7. The Horror Of It All: Stories (2025)
8. Beneath a Dying Sun: Western Short Stories (2025)
9. Beneath a Dying Son: New Testament Short Stories (2025)
10. grenade (2025)

HOLY ACHE
OF THE
UNBECOMING
LAUGHTON J. COLLINS, JR.

HOLY ACHE
OF THE
UNBECOMING

LAUGHTON J. COLLINS, JR.

HOLY ACHE
OF THE
UNBECOMING

LAUGHTON J. COLLINS, JR.

My Website

Social Media

Link Tree

dot.profile

Authors Den

Goodreads

Amazon Author Page

Bookwire

Substack